Trick of the Light

Trick
of the Light

MARINA COHEN

Koven, — Don't be fooled. Marina Cohen 04/08

Vanwell Publishing Limited

St. Catharines, Ontario

Vanwell Publishing acknowledges the financial support of the
Government of Canada through the Book Publishing Industry
Development Program for our publishing activities.

Vanwell Publishing acknowledges the Government of Ontario through
the Ontario Media Development Corporation's Book Initiative.

Vanwell Publishing Limited
1 Northrup Crescent, P.O. Box 2131
St. Catharines, Ontario L2R 7S2
tel: 905-937-3100 • fax: 905-937-1760
1-800-661-6136
sales@vanwell.com

Cover Illustration by Craig Howarth

Printed in Canada

Library and Archives Canada Cataloguing in Publication

Cohen, Marina
Trick of the light / Marina Cohen.

ISBN 978-1-55068-982-2

I. Title.

PS8605.O378T75 2007   jC813'.6   C2007-905900-7

For my parents,
Barbara and Joe Crifo.

ACKNOWLEDGEMENTS

Many thanks to all the wonderful people who helped make this novel the best it can be, including my mentor, Marsha Skrypuch, for her support and guidance; Private Kidcrit readers: Elizabeth B, Mary B, Christine Barkey, Hélène Boudreau, James Bow, Anita Daher, Amy Dupire, Veronica G, Rose Holck, Loraine Kemp, Janet McConnaughey, Lari Tanner and especially Helaine Becker and Martha Martin who read the entire manuscript and provided excellent feedback; my esteemed colleague, Joni Miyata, for lending me her eagle eyes; Craig Howarth for his amazing artwork; and to Renée Giguère for her skills as a designer.

Thanks to my husband, Michael Cohen, without whose love and support this project would never have been possible.

Thank you also to Angela Dobler, managing editor at Vanwell Publishing.

A very special thank you to my editor, Fiona Lamb, for her constant enthusiasm, expert feedback and tireless patience.

A heartfelt thanks to the staff at Vanwell Publishing and to my publisher, Ben Kooter, for once again believing in my writing.

chapter one

Drake Livingstone licked the flap of the large manila envelope and sealed his fate inside. He grabbed a handful of stamps—all he could find— and pasted them in the upper right hand corner. He ran a fingertip over the name he'd scrawled across the front.

You're my last hope, he thought.

Drake had to be quick. His parents scrutinized his every move. For the past ten months, they thought he'd gone crazy. They even had the nerve to send him to a psychiatrist.

"For zee hundredz time, Zelma is a figment of your imagination," said Dr Gügenheimer-Schultz.

"*Stella*," said Drake.

"Vat?"

"Her name is *Stella*."

The doctor's beady eyes narrowed. He scribbled furiously into his notepad.

Great, thought Drake. *I'm already crazy— might as well add argumentative to the list.*

"As I vas saying, zis Sally does not exist. Your brain zimply invented her to compensate for all zee qualities you lack—hence, zee ultimate in twin complex."

"*Huh?* Look Doc, seems to me *you're* the one lacking—in *brains!*"

The doctor frowned and began scribbling again.

Fine. Write whatever you want. Rude. Confrontational. Toss in hostile for good measure.

Unfortunately, Drake's parents believed Gügenheimer-Schultz. They began talking to Drake like he was three years old. They wouldn't let him use knives anymore—not even plastic ones—and made him keep the door to his bedroom open at all times. The only place he was allowed to be alone was the bathroom and even there, not for very long.

"Taking a shower!" he hollered down the stairs.

Drake turned on the tap and yanked the curtain shut. Leaving the water running, he sneaked out of the bathroom, closing the door behind him. This would buy him some time, though not much.

Drake crept down the stairs. As his parents sat glued to the evening news, he clicked open the deadbolt and slipped out the front door.

The late October air was saturated with the scent of fall. Chimneys of nearby houses puffed the musky odor of burning wood into the night sky. Drake inhaled deeply as he hurried along the sidewalk. Cold drizzle numbed his face. A gust of wind scattered leaves and debris. He drew the precious envelope close to his chest so that the address would not smudge. *39 Pine Valley Drive.* It was only a thirty minute drive away, but it might as well have been halfway round the world.

The streetlamps had been lit since dinner time. Their amber glow tossed shadows over the houses and street. Out of the corner of his eye, Drake studied each and every one. He knew all too well what lurked in the shadows.

As he passed the dark school, a rustling in the bushes snatched his attention. Drake stopped so abruptly he nearly tipped forward. Catching his balance, he froze. Only his eyes moved as he inspected the shrubs that still clung to a smattering of brown, crusted leaves.

Something was in there.

He held his breath and waited. His grip on the envelope tightened, crushing the contents. As the dried leaves crinkled and crunched, Drake's thoughts raced. *Are they back? Are they after me?*

His heart hammered against his ribs. He was about to turn back, when the branches parted and a skunk scurried out. It crossed the street just ahead of him and disappeared under a neighbor's porch. Drake breathed a sigh of relief.

Only a stupid skunk, he thought. *I used to be afraid of skunks.* That fear seemed ridiculous to him now, after all he'd been through.

The mailbox wasn't far ahead. It stood like a lone tin soldier guarding the park. Light from a streetlamp cast a lean shadow that extended from the base of the mailbox halfway through the park. He noticed other shadows trailing from tree trunks, the park swing and slide.

Drake searched the sky. The moon was nowhere to be seen. The streetlamp was the only light source. All shadows should have led *away* from it...and yet...

Something was wrong.

A thin maple produced a shadow that stretched in the opposite direction from the others. It leaned *toward* the light, not *away* from it. The shadow was thicker than the tree trunk. Thicker and shaped like a...

Impossible, thought Drake. *Unless...*

Drake's heart leapt into his throat. He had to make a break for it. It was his only chance. If anything happened to him it wouldn't matter so long as the package left his hands.

Drake tucked the envelope under his arm like a football. He charged toward the mailbox, a running-back heading for the goal line. His strides fell heavy and fast, his rubber soles sucking the concrete.

The shadow shifted.

Panic gripped Drake. He lost his footing but quickly regained his balance. He tripped again. This time, he wasn't so lucky. His body lurched too far forward and he skidded face-first along the slick surface. He scraped his hands and cheek and fumbled the package. The envelope skipped off the sidewalk and came to a halt in the wet grass. Drake scrambled to his feet and scooped it up.

Then he smelled it—the stench of rotting meat.

It's over, he thought.

In the same instant, the shadow peeled itself off the ground. Arms formed, reaching toward Drake with sprouting claws. A tattered hood surrounded a faceless chasm, where only two black eyes protruded.

Fear flashed through Drake's veins like an electrical shock. It was painful and energizing at the same time. He knew this figure. He'd seen it before.

With every ounce of strength in him, he pushed his body toward the mailbox, racing against the shadow that slithered close behind. Twenty feet. Ten feet. He felt its icy breath prickle the back of his neck.

Drake stretched his arm out as far as he could. With his body still in forward motion, he managed to open the slot and fire his package inside. The hinges creaked and a thud echoed through the park as the heavy door slammed shut nearly severing his fingers in the process.

"Touchdown!" he yelled up into the night. Droplets of rain dripped down from his hair. The water mingled with the blood now seeping from his scrape.

The shadow could take him now. It didn't matter anymore. He turned to face his enemy; his arms stretched high in a mocking surrender.

A blast of wind rushed past him spraying his face with drizzle.

The sidewalk was empty.

He searched the street and the park. They were vacant as well. All shadows appeared normal once again.

Could I have imagined it? Am I as crazy as everyone thinks?

He shook his head. *It's a trick. They'll be back.*

He took a deep breath and started toward his house, his eyes fierce and resolute.

In front of the school, the bushes rustled again. "Stupid skunk," he spat, pausing to see if the animal would dare show itself a second time.

The rustling stopped and as Drake turned, velvety blackness draped over him like a cloak. It swallowed him in its empty folds and melted into a crack in the cement.

Wind whistled through the empty street.

chapter two

"Sheeerrrmaaan!" screeched the all too familiar voice. "Sheeerrrmaaan! Get down here this instant!"

What now? he sighed. *I've already done my homework, practiced violin for almost three hours, cleaned my room—what more could that woman possibly want?*

"Coming!" he yelled down the stairwell.

Ignoring his mother, tuning her out, playing dumb—he'd tried it all before. It was only delaying the inevitable. Much easier to just get things over with. The stairs groaned under his weight.

Shirley Glutz sat on the sofa in front of a thirteen-inch television. She didn't believe in what she referred to as the "brain-sucker", but she made an exception for the evening news.

"Sheeerrrmaaan!" she squealed.

"No need to shout. I'm right here."

Without so much as a sideways glance at him, Sherman's mother aimed the remote at the TV and turned up the volume to an excruciating level. "Listen!"

"*...Amber alert continues for missing twelve-year-old last seen five days ago. It is believed that the youth may have run away, as no evidence of abduction has been uncovered, though foul-play is not being ruled out...*"

A photograph of Drake appeared on the tiny screen. Sherman squinted to make out the face. The recognition hit him like a fastball square in the jaw and his knees buckled. He sunk to the sofa beside his mother. His stomach bottomed out.

"It's that Livingstone boy," said Mrs Glutz. "Our old neighbor from Cedar Grove. You know — your *friend!*"

The word *friend* shook him from his trance. Sherman had spent most of his life friendless. Drake had been his one and only friend—*if* you considered a crazy guy with a bizarre fixation a friend.

Last January Drake had lost his marbles; started claiming he had a twin sister who disappeared into the light of a solar eclipse. He kept badgering Sherman, trying to convince him that he had been sucked into some other world and that Sherman had gone with him. Even wackier, Drake claimed that they had left his sister, Stella, behind.

Riiiiight. Like Sherman's life was so crammed with unbridled excitement he could afford to forget an adventure like that. Violin practice, day in, day out—how thrilling.

"...youth had been under psychiatric care..."

Yup. Drake was a real looney-toon. Yet, sadly, this looney-toon had been his only friend. Even now, two months into his new school, Sherman was still an outcast among the local kids.

"...Drake Hamilton Livingstone is approximately five-foot-two, medium build, with short, sandy hair and dark brown eyes..."

Sherman's mother put a hand to her chest as though she were having a heart attack. "How dreadful!" she panted. "That boy's parents must be sick with worry! Oh Sherman, it could have been you!"

An Academy Award-winning performance, he thought.

"It's okay, Mom. I'm right here. I'm not going anywhere."

A wacky mother. A crazy friend—crazy missing friend, he corrected his thoughts. Good thing he and his dad were sane and accounted for.

* * *

Sherman's dad, Mortimer, stood over the ten-gallon tank in his study, holding Gertrude, his Chinese mantid. As Sherman entered the study, the seven-inch praying mantis cocked her head toward him a full 180°. It gave him the creeps even though he'd seen her do it a million times.

As Mortimer turned to face Sherman, his smile morphed into a look of concern. "What's wrong, son?"

"It's Drake, Dad," said Sherman, watching as his father returned the alien-looking insect to her hot and humid home. "He's missing. It was on the news."

"Missing? The Livingstone boy?" Shock rippled across his face. Instinctively he reached for Sherman. "That's terrible! Are you all right?"

Sherman stepped back. He took a deep breath and shook his head. "I don't think so. I mean, Drake was strange—definitely odd—but he was my *friend*."

Each time Sherman repeated the word, he felt a churning in the pit of his stomach. It was as

19

though something squashed deep within him was bubbling to the surface.

"Did they say how long he's been gone? Do they think he's been kidnapped?"

"Five days. They think he may have run away." Sherman's mind began to wander. *Where would Drake go? Is he still looking for the phantom-Stella?* Sherman's stomach felt like a geyser. It was going to explode.

"What can we do?" asked his father. "Should we call his parents? Is there anything you remember about your friend that might help them find him?"

Sherman's face turned gray. He bolted from the study, raced up the stairs and collapsed on the bathroom floor. He was going to be sick.

Cold sweat oozed from his body as the room began to spin. The sounds of the television, his parents' alarmed voices and their footsteps racing up the stairs merged into a kaleidoscope of clatter hammering in his ears. His eyesight dimmed, brightened, then dimmed again. A million tiny dots flickered in front of him like swarming fireflies.

What's happening? he thought. *What's wrong with me?* He heaved and gagged as his stomach lurched but nothing came up. Not so much as a burp. As his parents burst through the door the room suddenly settled. His eyes focused and the drumming in his ears ceased.

"Sherman," gasped his mother, kneeling beside him, "are you all right? Morty! Get him some water!"

"I'm fine," said Sherman, rising to unsteady feet. "I don't know what happened. I thought I was going to throw up. But it passed. I'm fine. Really." He dragged his sleeve across his damp forehead.

"Let me see your hands!" demanded his mother, pulling them forward to inspect his fingers. "Did you hurt your hands when you fell? Can you still play the violin? Oh please tell me you still can *play!*"

"My *hands* are fine," Sherman snapped, yanking them from her grasp. "I need to go to bed. Need to rest."

"That's right, Sherman," said his father. "You go to bed early. Try not to worry about Drake…" Then frowning at his wife he added, "And don't think about the violin. Just get some rest."

"Yes, Sherman," agreed his mother. "The Livingstone boy is fine. I'm sure of it. And you can think about your violin all day tomorrow."

Sherman and his dad exchanged hopeless glances. His father walked him to his bedroom and gave him a gentle hug, whispering in his ear, "Are you sure you're okay?"

Sherman nodded. He managed a half-hearted smile. He was about to close the door when his mother called over her shoulder.

"Oh Sherman, I almost forgot. Something came for you in the mail today. A package. Have you been ordering junk from eBay again?"

chapter three

Sherman stretched across his bed dangling his feet over the edge. He hadn't been expecting a package.

His eyes tapered suspiciously as he turned the wrinkled and water-stained envelope over in his hands. There was no return address. His name was little more than a smudge.

The postal worker who sorted this must have ESP, he thought, straining to decipher the address that had been his home for only four short months: *39 Pine Valley Drive.* It certainly came to the right place.

Sherman yawned as he checked the stainless steel clock hanging above the desk in his bedroom. It read twenty past seven, but that wasn't the only story it told. Beneath the Roman numeral twelve was a cut-out in the shape of a semi-circle. It was like a window into another universe blinking with stars. The timepiece was equipped with a rare mechanism and when accurately set, an image of the moon appeared and disappeared from the window according to its precise phase. The slice of light presently visible meant the moon had just entered its *New Crescent* phase.

Sherman returned his focus to the package in his hands. He paused for another moment and then tore at the flap. The contents spilled onto his bed and he scrambled to a sitting position.

A crumpled letter in the same scrawl, an old book, and a girl's necklace bounced to a halt on his lumpy quilt. He grabbed the necklace. A black stone hung suspended from a thin gold chain.

Why in the world would someone send me this? he wondered. Sherman lifted the letter warily. The signature leapt at him, drawing his eyes like a magnet. It was signed:

Your friend,
Drake

For the second time that evening, Sherman's thoughts spun in one direction, while the room whirled in the other. *Is this a clue to Drake's whereabouts? Should I tell Mom and Dad? Call the police?*

Sherman swallowed. He wished he was standing on some wooden stage in a hollow old theater gliding his bow in a perfect rendition of Bach's Partita in D major. *That* he could handle. *That* was easy. This was...*eerie*.

He decided it best to have a look at the letter before making any rash decisions. As his eyes ran the length of it, the words danced on the page, slipping in and out of focus. Sherman scrunched his eyes and took a deep breath. When he looked at the paper again, everything fell into place.

Dear Shermanosaurus,

Why in the world does he keep calling me that? thought Sherman.

You told me once you were a genius. Okay, Mr Genius, you're my last hope. The shadows have been acting weird lately. I think they're after me. Stella tried to warn me. She left me her diary, but I just can't figure it out. She wrote the whole *thing the night before we went through the light of the solar eclipse. It was like she was in some kind of a trance. I'm pretty sure the book holds the secret to getting her back. It's all up to you now, dude. Give it your best.*

Your friend,
Drake

The paper slid from Sherman's grasp and floated to the floor as he caught the last sentence:

P.S. I think he's back.

A shiver inched up Sherman's spine. He didn't like the sound of that last line. Who was *he*? And where was *he* back from?

One thing was certain, and that was if Drake were ever found, this letter was evidence enough to lock him up in the Looney Bin and throw away the key. It was one thing to dream up a twin sister. After all, lots of kids have imaginary friends, but the stuff about shadows being after Drake was super weird. Paranoid. Delusional.

Sherman flopped back on his bed wondering what to do. Tell Mom? Not a chance. Tell Dad? Good idea. Dad would know what to do. He was an entomologist. A scientist. He always kept a clear, analytical head.

Sherman bent to pick up the letter. He was about to head toward the door when he remembered the diary. He hadn't even looked at it. Maybe it contained an explanation or, at the very least, more information.

Sherman returned to his bed and grabbed the thin book. It looked pretty old. The faded, rust-colored cover was worn thin in the corners. It was bound textbook style, with the pages sewn right in. *They don't do that anymore, do they?* he wondered.

Sherman opened the cover and on the first page was one single entry. It was written in Drake's practically illegible writing.

I hate diaries!

So much for a clue. Why would Drake send him a diary saying he hated diaries? This was getting weirder by the minute.

Sherman flipped the page. What he saw left him ice-cold.

```
ooooo oo ooo ooooo

ooo o

ooooo o

o oooooooo oo oooooo

ooooooo ooooo oooo

ooooo oooooooooo oooooooo ooooo oo
oooo ooo ooooooooooo ooo oooo
oooooo oooo oo ooooo oo oo ooooooo

ooooooo ooooo o ooooo oooooooo o
ooo ooooooooooo oo ooooooo oooooo o
oooooooooo

ooooo oooooooooo oooooooo ooooo oo
oooo ooo ooooooooooo ooo ooooooooo
ooooooooo oooo oo ooooo oo oooooooo
ooooooo oooooo oooooo o ooo o  oo
```

The entire page, top to bottom, was nothing but random groupings of tiny circles. Like zeros. Sherman ran a trembling hand over the writing.

Whoever had written in the book must have pressed very hard, as the paper dipped and rose like Braille. Sherman's hands shook as he peeled back another page. Then another. And another. They were all filled with circles. Nothing but circles.

If the letter hadn't convinced him, the journal surely had.

"He's off the deep end!" gasped Sherman.

Sherman's mind was made up. Best take everything to his father and have him sort things out with the police.

Sherman gathered the envelope, the pendant, the letter and the diary. He was two steps out the door when a blinding flash from behind stopped him in his tracks. He swung around.

Something as powerful as lightning had lit up his room.

Stepping as lightly as his body would allow, Sherman moved one foot, then the other, until he could see into his bedroom. It was exactly as he'd left it. Messy as ever. His bed lay unmade. Books all over the floor. The poster of Mozart, his favorite composer, eyed him smugly from the wall opposite his bed. His Moon Phases clock ticked away. Beneath it, his paper-strewn desk lay in its usual disarray, with his trusty computer perched amidst the messy heap.

Flash! His bedroom exploded again with light.

Everything dropped from Sherman's hands. On his computer screen was a giant glowing head with a grotesque blue face, lightning-bolt hair and white pupil-less eyes.

Sherman stood perfectly still in the doorway. The laser-beam eyes searched and found him.

"Sheeerrrmannn! I once gave you a task to complete. Now I give you another—solve the riddle at hand!" Its voice was like a metallic hum.

Sherman felt like a suit of armor. Heavy and hollow. He didn't blink. He didn't breathe. He just watched in horror as the strange voice droned on: "She needs you. One last time."

There was a sizzling zap. The head disappeared from the computer screen and in the same instant the power in the entire house went out. Sherman teetered.

"Sheeerrrmaaan!" His mother's voice bellowed up from the dark hallway. "What are you up to? Did you blow a fuse?"

His body hit the floor with a dull thud.

"Sheeerrrmaaan? What's happening up there? Are your hands all right? Did you hurt your hands?"

Sherman lay on the floor in total darkness.

chapter four

The school bus jostled its passengers along the potholed side-road toward Aurora Middle School. *Seatbelts ought to be mandatory,* thought Sherman, as he felt his breakfast rise and fall with each jiggle, joggle and bump.

He hadn't slept a wink the night before and now exhaustion and nausea were battling for control of his body.

"Whacha got there, Squirmin?"

Sherman shoved the pendant in his pocket and snapped the diary shut. He turned to face the big kid leaning over his shoulder. He scowled. "If you choose to address me, kindly use my given name and not some travesty that serves to amuse no one but yourself."

"Ah, come on Vermin. Don't be so touchy." The bully grinned and punched him in the arm. "'Sides, it amuses lots of people. Really."

Sherman couldn't decide what was worse. At

his old school, except for Drake, he had been totally ignored. At his new school, he got plenty of attention, though not of the positive sort. For instance, Sherman's name endured relentless abuse: Squirmin, Squirmy, Vermin, Wormin, and Worm were the top contenders. His surname suffered similarly. Klutz, Mutts, Guts—and the particularly offensive but popular—Butts. After two months of name-assault, Sherman was starting to gain a deeper appreciation for what Drake had called him. At least *Shermanosaurus* had a nice ring to it, not to mention an air of strength and ferocity.

Billie thumped Sherman between the shoulders. "Earth to Wormin! Come in Wormin!"

Normally, Sherman was able to ignore Billie's taunts, but having spent all night awake trying to figure out the mysterious diary, his patience had worn thin. He took a long-drawn breath and fought back.

"Don't you have anything better to do, Billie—like harass some innocent kindergarten kid?" he muttered through clenched teeth. He tucked the diary safely into his backpack.

"Newp. I'm all yours!"

Billie ruffled Sherman's hair so that he looked like a pineapple. Sherman sighed and patted it smooth. It was so unfair. He considered himself a pretty nice guy. A pacifist. Kept to himself. Bothered no one. Yet, for some reason, the toughest, meanest, most merciless bully in the entire school had singled him out as *her* favorite target.

Wilhelmina Binkleburg, better known as Billie (or as Sherman liked to think of her—*The Beast),* smiled, revealing a mouth full of metal. She batted her eyes with exaggeration, her stringy, reddish-brown hair framing her square face. Then she bounced her basketball off the back of Sherman's head.

"Leave me alone," said Sherman, his eyes shooting daggers at her. He turned to face forward, refusing to give Billie any further satisfaction.

As the bus continued its perilous jaunt, Sherman willed his thoughts to more important matters. He summed up the facts in his mind:

1. *Delusional Drake, with non-existent twin*
2. *Drake's disappearance*
3. *Mysterious letter, asking for help*
4. *Diary full of nothing but circles*
5. *Giant head of light, living in my computer*

Sherman could have handled the first four. It was the last item that bothered him the most. Either he, Sherman, was as wonky as Drake, or

33

(and given recent events he had to consider this option), Drake wasn't so crazy after all. Either way, Sherman decided he couldn't tell a living soul about the package, at least not until he'd cracked the diary code. He needed to figure out what was in the diary—for his sake as much as for Drake's.

He pulled out the book and ran his hand over the faded cover. "If I could just figure it out…" he mumbled to himself.

The bus lurched to a halt in front of the school, ending the morning's daily near-death experience. Sherman waited patiently for everyone to exit, mulling over possible solutions to the code in his head. He was about to stand up when Billie leaned over his seat and whispered something in his ear.

"Binary System."

Sherman's head spun round so quickly it nearly twisted right off. "*What?* What did you just say?"

"Binary System." Billie's grin caught the sunrise, nearly blinding Sherman. "Used in computer programming…"

"I know what a *Binary System* is, you imbecile. *Why* did you just say it?"

"That's what's in the book you got there…"

Sherman's cheeks flushed a deep scarlet. What business did Wilhelmina Binkleburg have snooping

34

in his private affairs? It was one thing to bug him, call him names, use him for target practice, but who gave her the right to *spy* on him?

"...either that, or maybe some old World War II code. Both the Axis and Allies used codes, you know?"

"I...fully aware of what...codes...Wars..." Sherman was clearly flustered.

"Da Vinci used mirror script as his code. But I think whacha got there, Squirmy, is a Binary System."

Anger bubbled beneath Sherman's skin. "The Binary System uses zeros *and* ones! There are only zeros... Oh, never mind!"

Sherman flapped his hand in the air as though he were swatting a mosquito. He grabbed his backpack and stomped down the aisle of the bus. Billie stuck to him like gum on his shoe. As they stepped onto the concrete platform, he turned to face the girl who was a full three inches taller than him.

"Look, my book isn't any of your business. So, although I *really* appreciate your feeble attempt at assistance, I'd prefer it if you'd just make like a tree and *leave!*"

Billie ignored his last statement. She poked him hard in the belly. "Course...you know, Worm...

now that I think of it, Ralph always says…"

"Who in the world is *Ralph?*"

"Ralph? Oh, he's my brother," said Billie following Sherman into the schoolyard. "Like I was saying, Ralph says that a code is only as good as its creator…"

"*Really?*" scoffed Sherman. "And what exactly does *Ralph* know about codes?"

"Ralph works for CSIS. He's always crackin' codes and…"

"Your brother works for CSIS? Canadian Security Intelligence Service? The Canadian equivalent to the CIA? You've *got* to be kidding! How old is he, anyway? Fifty?"

"Thirty-six," said Billie. "Generation gap."

Sherman was skeptical. "What does he do for CSIS?"

"Well, he's really a mathematician I guess, but they use him for codes, you know. It's all about patterning, isn't it? Anyway, Ralph says to figure out yer code, you gotta figure out the code-creator."

"*Figure out the code-creator?* What's that supposed to mean?"

"You know, get inside their head." Billie put an index finger to her temple. "See what makes 'em tick. That sort of thing." She winked and nodded.

Wilhelmina Binkleburg was as articulate as

a baboon, and yet Sherman hated to admit she was making a lot of sense. He was going about this all wrong. He was looking at the code in isolation. If he wanted to figure it out he had to look toward the source. The source was Drake. What, exactly, did he know about Drake Livingstone?

* * *

Sherman yawned frequently throughout the morning activities. Lucky for him, they were working on algebra. He could solve algebraic equations in his sleep. He peered over at Billie and a sparkle of delight flared in his eyes. She seemed to be sweating over the simple computations.

At recess, Sherman brought out a pen and notebook. He nestled up against the chain link fence at the back of the schoolyard. He wrote Drake's name in bold capital letters in the center of the back page, then circled it three times. From the circle he drew arrows outward, brainstorming ideas.

Same age as me. Taller. Thinner. Likes sports. Basketball's his favorite. Talks about twin sister who doesn't exist. Stella. Why call her Stella? Why not Susan, or Sarah, or Brittany? Says we went through the light. The light of the eclipse. There was an eclipse. Total eclipse. That was in

January. It was after the eclipse that he started talking about Stella. Stella. It all comes back to the eclipse…eclipse…eclipse…

Sherman had written the word three times when a football landed smack in his lap, sending his pen and notebook flying. The football bounced up and hit him in the nose. A searing pain forced his hands to his face. He felt a warm, sticky wetness. It was blood.

Great! Just great! he thought. He closed his eyes, tilted his head backward and pinched his nose. He could taste the blood trickling down his throat.

"Who's Drake?"

Sherman opened his eyes. Billie stood above him holding her football in one hand and his notebook in the other.

"Not you again!" Sherman glared up at the pair of roguish green eyes. "You gave me a nosebleed!"

"Oh, suck it up, Mutts. Don't be so fragile." Billie reached into her pocket and handed Sherman a wad of what looked like semi-used tissues. "You know, there's a kid by the name of Drake. Fell off of the face of the Earth. Been all over the news."

Sherman slapped her hand away.

She shrugged her shoulders and stuffed the tissues back into her pocket. "Suit yourself."

"Just leave me alone, Billie. Is that so much to ask for?"

Billie ignored him as usual. "You interested in eclipses? You know, there was a total eclipse back in January…"

Sherman sighed. A few drops of blood sprayed from his nose. He snatched his notebook from Billie's grasp, tucked it under his arm and pulled himself up.

"Roger says it was a super-rare eclipse—heard of nothin' like it before."

"And who, pray tell, is *Roger?*" asked Sherman. "My brother."

"You said your brother's name was Ralph!"

"That's my other brother. This one's Roger."

"And what's he? An astronaut?"

"Good one, Worm!" Billie punched him in the arm. "Nah. He's an *astronomer*. He works for CASCA."

Sherman choked. "The Canadian Astronomical Society—Société Canadienne d'Astronomie?"

"Yeah! That's it!" Billie spiraled the football into the air and caught it with one hand. "Nice French accent. You're pretty smart, you know."

Sherman rolled his eyes. "Gee, thanks." Somehow compliments from *The Beast* who had nearly broken his nose weren't exactly welcome.

He narrowed his eyes. "Your brothers must be exceptionally intelligent. So, what happened to you?"

Billie's eyes narrowed. She smiled. "I think I'm startin' to like you, Germ!"

Wonderful. Just what my bruised body needs—more attention from Billie Binkleburg, thought Sherman, rubbing his nose.

The bell rang. Still clutching his nose with one hand and his notebook with the other, Sherman bulldozed past a beaming Billie and entered the school.

As the rest of the class droned through the afternoon lessons, Sherman held the diary under his desk. He examined it page by page. Nothing jumped out at him, only that the number of circles increased and decreased in no obvious pattern. Then, just as Sherman was about to shove the diary into his desk, he noticed something jammed between the pages and the spine. As best he could tell, it was a metal rod.

With the teacher's back to the class, Sherman risked holding the book up to the light. Whatever it was, it gleamed. He couldn't quite get his finger into the tiny space to pry it loose, so he shook the book hard and was about to whack it against his thigh. It slipped from his grasp and flew through the air landing with a slap on the floor right in front of Billie's desk. The rod jarred loose and rolled onto the floor.

It was a thin, gold pen.

chapter five

Billie picked up the pen and examined it.

"Give it to me," mouthed Sherman, stretching out his hand across the aisle of desks. Billie flashed him a devilish grin and shook her reddish-brown mop.

"I said, give it to me," Sherman whispered. Billie dangled the pen between her finger tips swinging it like a pendulum.

She's not going to get away with this! In one swift motion Sherman lunged at her. He grappled for the pen with outstretched arms, but she was able to stave off the assault with her free hand.

"Give...it...*over!*" Sherman snarled through clenched teeth. His arms flailed wildly, but he managed to seize a piece of the pen.

Billie yanked her hand away. Sherman threw himself at her, tipping Billie's chair with Billie still in it. The two hit the floor with a tremendous crash.

The class went wild. Jeers and laughter filled the room. Half the class stood up to get a better look. One girl looked like she was going to cry.

"Whooweee!" yelled the boy who sat in front of Sherman.

"This is better than Wrestling 24-7!" shouted another.

"Stop it! Stop it both of you!" said Ms Jacobs from the front of the class.

Sherman and Billie struggled with each other. They rolled right into a desk, spilling its contents onto the floor.

"I said STOP!" yelled Ms Jacobs, racing toward the commotion.

The pen slipped from Billie's grasp. Sherman tucked it into his pocket just as the teacher arrived on the scene.

"Billie!" scolded the teacher. "Are you picking fights again?"

Billie lay on the floor feigning a look of shock. "Who? *Moi?*" She batted her eyes insolently. The teacher frowned.

"Sorry Ms Jacobs. It's my fault," said Sherman lying on his back beside Billie. "My book. It slipped out of my hand." He rolled over and reached for the book, hugging it so that no attention would be drawn to it. "Billie was just helping me get my pen."

"Nice try," said Ms Jacobs. "Detention! Both of you!"

Billie grinned as she sprung to her feet. She held out a hand to help Sherman up.

* * *

"I woulda given it back, you know," said Billie as Sherman let the door swing back in her face.

Sherman stomped straight ahead refusing to look at Billie. They had been kept almost two hours after school, writing 200 lines:

> *I object to violence because when it appears to do good, the good is only temporary; the evil it does is permanent—Mahatma Gandhi.*

Sherman's wrist hurt even more than his pride.

The school bus was long gone. The sky was already a deep purple. The North Star was visible and so was the moon. A bitter wind whistled past Sherman and he shut his eyes as it lashed his face.

Sherman sighed and began the long walk home. Billie trotted along at his heels. Just his luck—she lived only three streets away from him.

"Come on, Squirmin," coaxed Billie, "let me have another look at that pen."

Sherman's indignation was firm and absolute. *Not on your life.*

"It's got somethin' to do with that code, doesn't it?"

Sherman pressed his lips tightly together. *I'm a vault.*

"Yer goin' to show me that pen, Germ," said Billie.

Sherman narrowed his eyes. *You think so?*

"Or…"

Billie smiled. Sherman saw the gleam in her eyes. His confidence teetered. Of all the Billie smiles Sherman knew, he hated this one the most. He braced himself.

"*Or*, I'm gonna tell your parents about yer code book. *And…*" she continued, "I'll tell 'em how you started a fist-fight with me—a girl—in class."

She might as well have kicked him in the stomach. He had planned on telling his parents he was late because he stayed for extra help. A little white lie. They wouldn't tolerate his getting a detention. And they certainly wouldn't tolerate him fighting with anyone, least of all a girl. His mother would go ballistic. She'd go on and on, ranting and raving about how he'd risked hurting his hands. His parents were sure to believe Billie too, with his swollen nose and all. Sherman sucked in a lungful of pre-winter cold.

"Fine, Billie. You win. But if I show it to you,

will you just leave me alone?"

"Sure," said Billie. "Sure I will."

Sherman thought her big teeth made her look like a crocodile. A crocodile with a lot of dental insurance.

Sherman dug deep into his pocket and pulled out the thin gold rod. It had the finest ballpoint tip he'd ever seen. As he held it up toward Billie, it sparkled in the moonlight.

"What's that?" asked Billie, reaching for it.

Sherman pulled it back. "What's what?"

"The inscription."

"There isn't any inscription," said Sherman turning it over in his hands.

"Sure there is. Hold it up to the light again."

Sherman sighed. Best humor *The Beast*.

He held the pen up and let it catch a sliver of moonlight. He was about to pull it back when his hand froze. Billie was right, there was something etched into the metal. Words coiled around the pen like a snake. He twisted it as he read aloud.

> *Written in the night*
> *When the moon is New,*
> *In the Full Moon's light*
> *All appears in view*

"It's a poem," said Billie, her green eyes sparkling. She reached for the pen. "I didn't see this on here before."

"It's a riddle," corrected Sherman pulling it out of her grasp. "And look," he tilted the pen away from the light. "It's only visible in the moonlight."

"Cool!" grinned Billie. "A magic pen! What's it say, again?"

Sherman volleyed the pen in and out of the light. He hated to admit it when Billie was right. "Magic," he muttered. His stomach began to bubble. That sick feeling was returning. The street and the houses began to spin.

"You okay?" asked Billie. It was the first time Sherman had seen a look of concern on Billie's face. It was out of place. Crocodiles never look concerned.

Sherman shook his head. "Going...to be...sick." He tucked the pen into his pocket and ran the rest of the way home.

* * *

That evening, Sherman lay on his bed. It had taken his stomach a while to settle. He hoped there'd be no more repeat episodes. As he held the pen up to the light, he examined it closely. The inscription was gone. He ran a fingertip over the

47

sleek surface. Neither an edge nor a bump to indicate anything was carved into it. He glanced at his clock—eight days until the full moon.

Sherman stood up and switched off the bedroom light. He drew open the heavy brocade drapes and let the soft glow of moonlight filter through the window. He held the pen up to the glass. As it caught the light, the inscription appeared anew.

He repeated the words over and over in his head. He knew what they meant, but he had to try it out to be sure. As he crossed the room and turned on the light, he cast a sideways glance at his computer screen. He was half-expecting it to spring to life with the talking luminescent head. *Solve the riddle at hand*, the head had instructed him.

The screen remained blank.

He approached the computer cautiously nonetheless, snatching a piece of paper from the printer tray as though it might at any moment sprout teeth and bite off his fingers.

He placed the paper on his desk and paused for a second to think. Then, he put pen to paper and began to write. *Billie Binkleburg has the brains of gelatinous zooplankton.* He felt the ballpoint glide effortlessly over the sheet, and yet the paper remained blank.

It was not a new moon.

"Just as I thought," said Sherman. "But to be sure, I need to wait."

He looked up at his trusty Moon Phases clock. Sherman had purchased it in a tiny souvenir shop in Switzerland when he had performed a violin solo at the International Festival of Youth Orchestras there. He hadn't exactly wanted to go, but his mother wouldn't have it any other way. As usual, he was at her mercy.

The Swiss shopkeeper had said the clock was *one of a kind*. It was really heavy, as though it were full of iron or something. Now that Sherman thought about it, there had been something oddly familiar about the shopkeeper. A strange flickering in her eyes that he swore he'd seen somewhere before.

Sherman shook off the feeling.

Eight days left, he thought, tucking the pen safely into the spine of the diary. He flipped through the pages once again, running his hand over the mysterious circles.

chapter six

The glowing circle of the moon ticked its way into the sapphire universe in Sherman's clock. It passed through First Quarter, then Waxing Gibbous until it finally reached the Full phase.

At school, Billie pestered Sherman relentlessly about the pen and the diary. Each time she mentioned it, he stonewalled her. But Billie didn't like to be stonewalled so this led to a series of *unfortunate accidents*. In the course of a week, Billie managed to serve a volleyball into his gut, spill a paint jar into his lap, fling a chalkboard eraser into his fruit cup, and deliver an endless series of arm punches and hair rufflings.

"You're a bully, Billie!" said Sherman, as they rode home on the school bus.

"Am not," she scoffed, leaning over his shoulder. "I like you, Klutz. Really. You don't bully someone you like, now do you?"

Sherman shuddered at the thought of what *The*

Beast might do to him if she actually *disliked* him.

"Look, I just live by Randy's philosophy," said Billie. "*Go hard. Or go home.* Randy's in the CFL."

"The Canadian Football League?" Sherman sighed. "Terrific. So, who's Randy—no wait—let me guess. Your brother."

Billie grinned. "Close."

"All right, Billie. So who is he?"

"He's my *step*-brother." Billie twirled her basketball on her fingertip.

Sherman rolled his eyes. Billie had a way of pushing his buttons. "Exactly how many brothers do you have?"

"Twelve."

"Twelve?" gasped Sherman.

"Three brothers, four half-brothers, five step-brothers... Blended family, you know."

"Twelve brothers? And you're the only..." Sherman searched for the right word, but when nothing came, he settled on, "*girl?*"

"Yup. That'd be me." She blinked more times than necessary.

No wonder she's so tough, thought Sherman.

"Look Billie, just stop liking me so much, all right? You're killing me!"

Billie gave a raspy chuckle. "You're too funny, you know that, Guts?" She flicked his ear. "So, when are you going to solve that riddle?"

"I solved it ages ago."

Billie dribbled her ball in the aisle.

"Really? So did I."

"Oh, you did?" said Sherman. "So, tell me then. What does it mean?"

Billie stopped dribbling and shook her head. "No dice. I'm not tellin' you, 'cause you don't really know, do ya?"

"What?" Sherman was indignant. "I do so!"

"Prove it. You tell me first and I'll tell you if you're right."

"That is the oldest trick in the book. Do you see an 'S' for *Stupid* tattooed across my forehead?"

Billie paused for a moment pretending to examine Sherman's brow. Sherman could almost feel the steam bursting through his pores.

"Okay," she said grinning. "Here's the deal. We'll both write down our answers and exchange them at the same time. That way I'll prove to you that I know the answer to yer riddle."

Sherman eyed Billie suspiciously.

"Fine."

He ripped out a page from the back of his notebook and tore it in half. He handed one piece to Billie and began to write on the other. When he finished writing, he folded the paper and handed it to Billie. She snatched it from his fingers and tossed her note into his lap.

"Ha!" she shouted. "Gottcha!"

Sherman opened Billie's paper. It read: *Sucker!*

"Brilliant, Billie. Just brilliant." Sherman's expression remained pokerfaced.

Billie unfolded the paper in her hands. Her grin dropped like a flapjack.

Sherman's note read: "You've got to wake up pretty early to fool the Shermanosaurus!"

"*Shermanosaurus?*" Billie wrinkled her nose.

"Whatever. Okay, you got me. I dunno what that riddle means. But if you tell me, I'll promise not to tell a soul about yer magic pen or the diary code. I've kept yer secret until now, haven't I?"

Sherman started to turn away.

She grabbed his shoulder.

"And…" she continued, "I'll stop buggin' you. Really. This time I swear."

Billie looked serious. Sherman knew he was going to hate himself, but he was thinking he just might trust Billie. He opened his mouth to speak, but the words stuck like postage stamps to the tip of his tongue.

Billie's eyes twinkled in anticipation. Something about her expression reminded him of a hound salivating after a thick and juicy steak.

"Forget it," he said finally. "I just don't trust you, Billie."

Billie looked hurt.

"Okay, Butts. I understand." She leaned back into her seat and stared silently out the bus window until her stop. Sherman tried to catch her eye before she left, but she exited without so much as a poke, punch or shove. She didn't even dribble her basketball down the aisle.

* * *

According to Sherman's clock, the moon entered its full phase that evening. He was itching to test his theory.

During dinner, Sherman sat deep in thought. *What secrets will the diary reveal? Will it lead me to Drake? Will it explain the sick feeling that keeps spinning my insides? Explain the glowing head living in my computer?*

His parents carried on their conversation as though he wasn't there.

"It's the *Greenhouse Effect,*" said Shirley Glutz through a mouthful of mashed potatoes.

"The Greenhouse Effect has nothing to do with it, my dear," said his father. "The Greenhouse Effect merely refers to the rise in temperature that the Earth experiences because certain gases in the atmosphere lock in energy from the sun. It has nothing whatsoever to do with volcanic eruptions."

"Oh, I beg to differ, Morty," said Sherman's mother pointing her fork at his father's nose. "What is inside a volcano?"

Sherman was only half listening. He knew the conversation would end up in one of his mother's circular arguments. He traced happy faces in his mashed potatoes with his fork.

"Lava," responded his father.

"Exactly." His mother shoved another heap of mashed potatoes onto her fork and into her mouth, after flashing his father a satisfied grin.

"I don't follow you, darling."

"Lava is hot."

"Quite. However, I fail to see the connection, Precious."

Sherman and his father were used to his mother's zigzagging train of thought. She could start off telling you about her trip to the supermarket to purchase plums and end up talking about the mating habits of the manatee. And the frustrating thing was, to her, these topics were perfectly related.

"Lava is hot. So is a greenhouse. They are both *hot*."

You seem to be missing the point, buttercup. Let me explain. To be precise, the Earth is not full of lava, but of molten rock, which is called *magma* while it is beneath the Earth's surface and *lava* once it escapes. When a lot of magma is sitting around in the magma chamber, it can cool off and release gases. These gases increase pressure inside the volcano. When the pressure becomes too great, the volcano erupts."

"A-ha!" she shouted reaching for the peas.

"Gases! You just said that *gases* cause the Greenhouse Effect and *gases* increase the pressure in the volcano. So, Morty, logic would dictate that volcanoes erupt as a result of the Greenhouse Effect. There you are. Now pass the roast beef."

Mortimer Glutz closed his eyes and let his breath whistle through his teeth. Somewhere there was a debating team missing its star.

He decided it best to let his wife think she was right. He changed the subject.

"Interesting how all these recent volcanic eruptions have occurred just prior to the lunar eclipse."

Sherman had tuned out most of the discussion. But the mention of an eclipse catapulted him into the conversation.

"Volcanic eruptions? A lunar eclipse? What?

When? Why haven't I heard of this?"

"Really, Sherman," scolded his mother. "You ought to make a point of being more informed. The eclipse has been all over the news. As well as all the volcanic eruptions. Absolutely devastated a number of already impoverished areas. It's like you've been in your own little world ever since the disappearance of that Livingstone boy. Speaking of which, has the poor fellow resurfaced yet?"

The truth was that Sherman *had* been in his own little world since Drake disappeared. It was a world full of gold pens and phantom twins and glowing heads. Not to mention books and books filled with nothing but circles.

Sherman sighed. "He's still missing."

"Dreadful. Just dreadful."

"When will the eclipse take place?" Sherman asked.

"Totality begins tonight, at approximately 1:17 a.m." said his father. "The moon will be hidden in the Earth's shadow for just over an hour. Shame we'll all be asleep. Lunar eclipses usually make the moon appear orange or red. This will be a rare eclipse. With all the recent volcanic activity, large amounts of volcanic ash present in the Earth's atmosphere will render the Moon virtually invisible."

Another eclipse? thought Sherman. *The Moon will disappear?*

The skin on the back of his neck prickled.

How could I have missed this?

chapter seven

A single ghostly figure stood swathed in radiance. Swirls of white light spun round her like threads of fine silk wrapping and blinding her in brilliance. Every color imaginable filtered through her as though she were a prism casting rainbows in all directions.

She stood alone at the base of the Crystal Obelisk. It was a beacon of hope. It was a tunnel of light.

He's been captured.

Yes.

What are we going to do?

Wait.

We can't just wait. We have to do something.

We shall. We shall let him take us.

Let him take us? You can't mean that!

I do.

But what will happen to my brother? To the light? To the universe?

Have faith in me. You have trusted me until now. Trust me a little while longer. It is almost over. You have done well.

chapter eight

Drake awoke from what felt like an endless sleep. His brain was hazy with half-thoughts. *Happened? Am I? Where?*

He groaned, shifting his cold, stiff body. His eyelids fluttered once or twice then opened.

Everything was black. Completely black.

He waited for his pupils to adjust to the darkness. Drake had an uncanny ability to see in the dark. There was a time when he took great pride in this mysterious ability. But that was before he knew where this power had come from.

Drake had been lying on a hard, icy surface and his whole body felt numb. As he pulled himself to a sitting position, sensation pulsed through him and his muscles ached. Wherever he was, it was colder than a meat freezer. His skin prickled beneath his clothing.

"Alas, you wake," said an iron voice. "Better for you, had you remained asleep."

Drake's heart leapt into his throat as his head snapped in the direction of the sound. *That voice! I know it!* He forced down the lump with a dry swallow.

Drake crouched back and realized he was lying alongside a wall. He pressed his weight against it.

As his eyes began to adjust, he could see shadows melting into one another. He saw contours. Silhouettes. Wispy movement. But nothing concrete. Not yet.

"How good of you to remember me," said the voice. "For a moment I thought you had forgotten."

Drake's eyesight sharpened. He could now make out the shape of a cloaked figure towering over him. Dead eyes, like those of a shark, fixed him with a cold stare, while a wide mouth smiled, revealing row upon row of black, razor-sharp teeth.

"*Umbra,*" Drake whispered.

"*Shadowmaster,* to you, my dear Drake. After all, we parted on, shall we say, more formal terms."

Memories collided in Drake's brain. He had encountered this monster before. He had defeated him. It was over. *Wasn't it?* He summoned every ounce of courage in him. His voice trembled.

"I th-thought you w-were...*dead.*"

"*Dead?*" Umbra's flat voice rose with a trace of amusement. "Driven away, perhaps, but far from dead, as you can see."

Drake swallowed. *Say something. Anything.*

"Why'd you bring me here? What do you want from me?"

"It is not *you* I want, it is...*her.* You see, it was because of you that I failed the last time. Now, it will be because of *you* that I succeed."

Drake placed a hand on the strange wall. It felt as smooth as polished metal. He drew himself up to unsteady feet.

"If you expect me to help you get her, you're wasting your time," he said, raising his chin. "You might as well kill me now."

Umbra extended a long limb with sharp claws protruding from bony digits.

"Drake, Drake. Why so dramatic? Had I wished to *kill you* I should have already done so. And, as for your helping me, why, my friend, you *already have.* A worm on the hook, and the big fish bites."

A frenzy of ghostly laughter erupted. The sound echoed, helping Drake get a better sense of his surroundings. He was in an enormous, empty chamber. Even with his keen night-vision, he

63

could see no end to it either up or across. Shadows slithered about the ground filling the chamber with the foulest of smells.

Shadowbands! Soldiers of darkness! He knew these creatures all too well!

Drake watched the phantoms slide like ribbons of black smoke toward the feet of their master. One of these fiends had stolen him from his world and had brought him here. *But how?* Bile rose in Drake's throat. *And why?*

Umbra addressed one of his minions, "Find Spinneret. Tell her it is time. Aura will surrender now that I have Drake."

The servant cackled in response then slipped beyond Drake's vision.

Who in the world is Spinneret? thought Drake. Once again, Umbra read his thoughts.

"Spinneret has many names. In your world she is known as Attercorpus Fimbriungus. But that would have been several hundred million years before your time..." he mused. "I must say, your sister will greatly enjoy making her acquaintance." Umbra's eyes narrowed to slits.

Drake, who had been pressed against the wall, now took a step forward. He knew he was no match for the cloaked monster but he had to think beyond his own safety.

"Leave Stella alone, Shadow-scum! She has nothing to do with you or this world!"

"Tsk. Tsk. Flattery will get you nowhere. And I'm afraid Stella has *everything* to do with it," sighed Umbra. "You see, Drake, I seek to destroy Aura, and Aura *is* Stella, and Stella is *Aura*. They are one and the same... At least, for *now* they are."

Drake didn't understand a thing. How had his twin sister's life become intertwined with the Source of Eternal Light, Aura? What *was* their connection? And why was the ancient creature of darkness out to destroy them both?

Thoughts whirled in Drake's mind, but he tried to smother them. Umbra could see inside him. Umbra could read his mind.

There was a time when Drake had been horribly jealous of his twin. Umbra had known his inner-most thoughts and had taken advantage of these feelings. He had used Drake as an instrument in his plan to destroy all light in the universe. Drake was even supposed to join him in his evil quest. Umbra proved this by showing Drake that the letters in his name, *Drake Livingstone*, also spelled *Evil Darking Stone*. He had used Drake to bring Stella to him.

Not again. Not this time. Drake searched the darkness. He could see no escape. Helplessness paralyzed him. He couldn't help Stella. He couldn't even help himself. He fell back against the wall and sunk to a squatting position. "How long have I been here?"

"In your time? Or ours?" Umbra ran a long claw along the side of his pointed chin.

"*Huh?*"

"A mere ten Earth days have passed, but here on the Halfstone it has been closer to thirty-nine years."

Drake choked. "Thirty-nine years! I've been *asleep* for thirty-nine years?"

"Technically, for you...I suppose."

"But, how can that be?"

"Drake," Umbra sighed. "Sleep has dulled your senses. You have forgotten much."

Umbra clicked his razor-sharp claws. "Time means nothing. It is all relative. You are no longer in your space—the Earth's space. You are in ours. That means you are no longer in your time, but ours. No longer in your present, but in *our present*. For you this is a time near the beginning of the universe."

Drake searched his memory.

What Umbra said was true. When he had traveled through the light in the solar eclipse, Drake had stayed on the Halfstone for what felt like an entire day. When he had returned home, only one minute had passed. He could live a lifetime on the Halfstone in one month of Earth time.

He ran his hands up over his face. Before the Shadowband had stolen him, he had cut his cheek on the sidewalk. There was no cut now. Not even so much as a scab remained. But he didn't feel older. He hadn't grown a beard like some sort of character out of a nursery rhyme. Had he aged *ten days? Or thirty-nine years?* It was all so confusing.

"The past is thin, Drake. It moves much quicker than the present. And, as you have already learned, if you alter the past, you alter the present. And the future." Umbra chuckled and the sound was as vile as fingernails running down a chalkboard.

Drake had once altered the past and it had cost him his sister. Now he had to figure out a way to change things again and bring her back. *But how?*

A thought leapt into Drake's brain before he could stop it. *Hopefully the package made it through.*

"Package? What *package?*" Umbra was no longer laughing.

Think. Think! Say something, quickly. Say anything…

"I want to join you!" Drake blurted out.

Umbra did not respond. His lifeless eyes fixed Drake with a searching stare that felt like bugs crawling all over his skin.

Drake cleared his throat.

"Really, I swear. I made a mistake the last time. A horrible mistake. I should have stuck with you, great Shadowmaster. I should never have betrayed you."

Umbra's stare remained suspicious.

Drake tried again. "You have to believe me. I *am*, after all, your *Evil Darking Stone*."

chapter nine

Sherman opened the drapes and gazed into the cloudless night. An enormous full moon hovered in a hazy glow.

He shifted the diary from one sweaty hand to another as he glanced over his shoulder at his Moon Phases clock. The sky in the clock matched the sky outside perfectly, like some eerie alternate universe. Even the constellations visible through his bedroom window appeared in the window of his clock. *Remarkable*, thought Sherman. *Must be what the Swiss shopkeeper meant when she said the clock was "one of a kind".*

Turning back to the window, he took a deep breath and opened the book.

In the Full Moon's light, all appears in view...

"This is it," he whispered.

Drake's entry glowered at him: *I hate diaries!*
Sherman sighed.

"I know exactly what you mean, buddy."

Sherman closed his eyes and with trembling fingers he opened the book to a page somewhere in the middle. His pulse quickened as his fingertips slid across the paper, rising and falling over the impressions. *Nothing but circles.*

Or should I say—full moons?

He tilted the book to catch the sun's light that reflected off the dark surface of the moon. He opened his eyes.

His breath caught in his throat as the dark etchings began to fade. Hidden beneath each tiny circle was a single dazzling letter. Sherman scrunched his eyes and opened them.

"Not a dream…" he whispered once he'd found his voice.

He scanned the page and what he read sent shivers rippling through his body. Though he wasn't quite sure what to expect, he thought he'd find diary entries with dates and times. This was nothing like it.

"This is no diary!" he gasped. "It's a…a…play! And what's more, I'm the—STAR!"

Sherman licked his cracked lips. Wide-eyed, he began to read:

TRICK OF THE LIGHT
Act 2
Scene 1

Sherman Glutz's bedroom

Sherman Glutz: *(He stands in front of a large window holding a faded book. A clock on the wall reads 6:30.)* This is it. *(He opens the book and sighs.)* I know exactly what you mean, buddy. *(He shuts his eyes and turns to the middle of the book, tilting it to catch the light.)* Not a dream. This is no diary! It's a...a...play! And what's more, I'm the—STAR!

Sherman's stomach lurched.

"This is totally insane! This is *me. Here. Now.* This just happened! How could anyone know? How could Drake or Stella or *whoever* have known?"

Sherman shook. Fear coursed through his veins. He suddenly felt like he was trapped in some horror story, like the *Goosebumps* books he used to read. He swallowed hard and read on.

Sherman Glutz: This is totally insane! This is *me. Here. Now.* This just happened! How could anyone know? How could Drake or Stella or whoever have known?

The book slid from Sherman's hands. It hit the floor at the same time as his body.

As he stared at the stucco ceiling the room began to spin. Round and round and round. A cramp seized his stomach—the strongest one yet. He panted as beads of sweat formed on his temples. There was a cannonball in Sherman's stomach and one way or another, it was coming out.

As he lay on his back gasping and coughing, the cannonball rumbled up through his innards, squished through his throat and exploded from his lips. For one brief second, the room was lit by a ball of glittering light! It burst into the air like a dazzling display of fireworks, only it wasn't fireworks—it was a ball of flashing fireflies! The glowing insects scattered and then vanished altogether, leaving Sherman lying in darkness. His eyes rolled to the back of his head and he slipped into unconsciousness.

chapter ten

Sherman awoke to the sound of his mother bellowing up the stairs, wondering, yet again, if he'd hurt his hands and reminding him he had a private violin lesson to prepare for. His thoughts were a blur.

He took a deep breath. As he exhaled, memories emerged from the back of his brain like a ship out of the fog. Not just any ship—a great ocean liner crammed with long suppressed images, feelings and experiences. It was all there. It came back to him like an old movie reel spinning inside his head.

Sherman bolted up. He snatched the book and turned to the very beginning. Holding the pages up to the light, he read:

TRICK OF THE LIGHT
Act 1
Scene 1

A sidewalk in winter.

Sherman Glutz: Ahem.

Drake Livingstone: *(swinging round to face him.)* Sherman, don't you know better than to sneak up on someone?"

Sherman Glutz: I wasn't *sneaking.* I was approaching in silence. There's a difference.

Drake Livingstone: Look Sher, I know you sent me the note.

Sherman Glutz: What note?

Drake Livingstone: Don't play games with me. I know it was you.

Sherman Glutz: I have no idea what you're talking about. I just wanted to tell you... *(his voice fades.)*

Drake Livingstone: Spit it out. I haven't got all day. *(Sherman clears his throat twice. Drake turns to leave.)*

Sherman Glutz: I'm going to get even with Parks.

Sherman's heart thumped against his ribs. *It's true. It's all true.* Everything that Sherman was reading had actually happened. Last January, he had played a trick on his substitute teacher, Miss Parks. He had brought in Gertrude and with Drake's help he had placed the seven-inch praying mantis on the teacher's desk in hopes to frighten her. Only she wasn't scared in the least.

Sherman skipped a few pages.

Miss Parks: *(Eyeing Sherman.)* Recess detention. *(She turns to face Drake.)* You as well, Drake.

Drake Livingstone: But I didn't...I had nothing to do with...it wasn't my...

Recess! How could he ever have forgotten *that* recess! Sherman turned the page.

Miss Parks: *(The teacher transforms into a human-fireball. Flames surround the classroom, burning as high as the ceiling.)* I am The Keeper of Earthly Light. In two days, darkness will envelope the universe. Unless Aura is saved, all will be lost.

Sherman realized he'd been holding his breath. He released the air trapped in his lungs and shook his head. *How could I have forgotten? It all happened. It really did.* Sherman remembered the flickering glow in Miss Park's eyes after she'd transformed back into herself.

"That flicker," he said to himself. "That was what I saw in the eyes of the Swiss lady who sold me the Moon Phases clock! She must have been the Earthly Keeper of Light in one of her disguises. So was that head in my computer—that was her too." He glanced over his shoulder at the timepiece that hung on his wall.

"Why did she make me buy that clock?" He bit his lower lip. The diary had answers. He turned back to the book and read on.

Scene 4

Drake and Sherman crouch in a stairwell facing the rear of the school. They are wearing Sherman-Shields—cheap sunglasses with film pasted over the lenses to protect their eyes from the impending eclipse.

Drake Livingstone: It's begun.
(Sherman nods. The sky slowly begins to transform. Darkness creeps across the sun and a shadow slides across the field. Just before the sun is completely swallowed, a figure appears in the

yard. It is Stella and she is racing across the field toward the opening in the fence. Drake and Sherman bolt out of the building to meet her. They duck into the woods and sprint toward the secret hollow to watch the eclipse.)

Sherman Glutz: Minutes until totality!
(Shadowy creatures appear slithering from tree trunk to tree truck. Sherman stumbles and falls. He is swarmed by dark limbs.) Help!

Drake Livingstone: Let's get outta here!"
(He tows Sherman to his feet and calls to Stella.) Wait up!

Sherman Glutz: Seconds until Baily's Beads! *(The moon slips over the remainder of the sun and the outer rim looks like a string of pearls as light shines through the lunar peaks and valleys. The necklace transforms into a diamond ring, then fades to crimson and then disappears to darkness...)*

Sherman steadied himself, letting everything gel in his mind. First a solar eclipse—now a lunar eclipse. Volcanoes are erupting. A strange clock with a window to the heavens ticks on his wall. A missing friend. Gold pen. Magic book.

Sherman looked down at the pages pressed between his hands. He realized with a shock:

"If Act 1 already happened...then what I do in Act 2 is the key to the future and the key to setting everything right."

chapter eleven

The phone rang five times before a familiar voice answered it.

"Hi, it's me," said Sherman, his voice sluggish and awkward. He had never read from a script before. "I, *er*, need your help."

There was a long pause on the other line. Sherman could just picture that old crocodile grin.

"Thought you didn't trust me, *Vermin?*"

Sherman gritted his teeth. He didn't. Plus, calling Billie was as good as apologizing and that made Sherman all the more irritated, seeing that if anyone should be apologizing, it should be *The Beast*, not him.

Sherman glanced at his clock. Time was running out.

"Okay, I trust you Billie. Are you happy?"

"Say it like you mean it."

"I don't have time for this, Billie. My friends' lives are hanging by a thread. Come to think of it, so is yours, and mine and everyone else's in the universe."

"Whoa, Squirmy!" Billie chuckled. "Whachou babbling about?"

"No time to explain. Not now, anyway. Can you meet me at the bus stop at the end of your street in ten minutes?"

Silence on the other end. Sherman wondered what Billie was thinking. According to what he'd read, she'd agree. He bit his lower lip just the same.

"See you in ten," she said finally.

This book is like a crystal ball, thought Sherman. He was about to hang up, when he remembered his last lines.

"Oh, and Billie? Wear dark clothes, and bring some sort of light."

* * *

Sherman sat at the bus stop, his violin case resting against his shins. He wished he didn't have to lug the darn thing along, but it was, as usual, his only means of escaping the watchful eye of his mother. *Hopefully Ms Wong got my message and won't call Mom to double check on why I cancelled my lesson.*

As he waited for Billie, Sherman thumbed through the next scene in the book. He shuddered at the thought of what lay ahead. *I could ignore it*, he thought, *throw the stupid book in the trash and pretend it never existed.* His shoulders sagged. *Never existed. Kind of like Stella. And now Drake.*

He took a deep breath. He couldn't let them down.

Sherman was about to read further when he saw Billie rounding the corner. She wore black jeans and a black ski jacket and even a black toque. Her pockets looked lumpy, all jammed up with something. She grinned and her braces twinkled in the moonlight.

"Hey Squirm. See you got your book there," said Billie. "Wanna tell me what's in it now?"

"Better sit down," he sighed. "It's a long story."

Billie took off her toque and plopped herself onto the opposite end of the wooden bench. She folded her arms, eyeing Sherman with a swirling mixture of curiosity, suspicion and delight.

Sherman started from the beginning. He stammered through the spectacular events that even he thought sounded totally absurd when spoken aloud. When he finished, Billie was silent for a minute. She chewed her thumbnail.

"Let me get this straight," she said finally. There was a hint of amusement lingering behind her frown. "All that crazy stuff happened—it *really* happened—and then you just *forgot about it?*"

Sherman winced. He couldn't tell if she believed him or was setting him up. Maybe she was humoring him. Suddenly, he knew how Drake must have felt all those months with everyone treating him like he was three cards short of a full deck.

"And now…" Billie continued, "now you want *me* to break into your friend's—*missing friend's*—house and steal his…his…*alarm clock?*"

Sherman raised his eyebrows and nodded feebly.

"Are you outta yer mind?"

"That is a solid possibility."

Billie rolled her eyes and shook her reddish mop.

"Well," she sighed, "if we get caught at least we'll have Rufus on our side—my brother in the CSC."

"Here we go with the brothers again. The CSC?"

"Correctional Services of Canada."

Great, thought Sherman. *I suppose it can't hurt to have the warden on your side.*

"You know, if I hadn't seen that magical inscription with my own eyes, Worm, I'd think you were bonkers."

Sherman's back straightened. "So you believe me?" he asked hopefully.

"I dunno," she said. "I'm, whadyacall, *reserving judgment.*"

Sherman nodded. *Reserving judgment* was good. It was more than he'd hoped for under the circumstances.

"Thing is, Squirmy, magic book or not, you can't travel through time," said Billie. "So, I still don't get how we're going to get Stella back."

"Why can't you?" asked Sherman. "You can travel through space, right?"

"That's different."

"Maybe. Maybe not," said Sherman. "Think about it. When you look up into space you can see stars shining. Stars that have burnt out millions of years ago. But you still see them, as though they're still alive. Here. And now. So, what if you could travel into that light?"

Billie was thinking so hard her face looked cramped. "You know," she said finally, "I think I get it. Even Roger says that the Hubble Space

Telescope has taken pictures of the very first galaxies—the first stars that got heated up right after the so-called *big bang*…that's crazy, eh?"

"No crazier than what we're about to do."

They exchanged worried glances.

"Lemme see that book," said Billie. "I wanna know exactly what I'm up against here."

Sherman watched as Billie opened the book. The full moon illuminated the page and it exploded once again with dazzling words. Her face contorted into various expressions of amazement as she read.

* * *

The bus screeched to a halt sounding like a wounded animal.

"Cedar Grove," said Sherman, stepping onto the sidewalk. "My old stomping ground."

"Doesn't seem like you done too much stompin'." Billie laughed, poking Sherman in his gut. He slapped her hand away and frowned indignantly.

Billie handed Sherman back his book. He made sure that the gold pen was still lodged in the spine and then he tucked it into his violin case.

"Are you good with the plan?" asked Sherman.

"Piece a cake," she shrugged.

Sherman and Billie strolled along the sidewalk trying hard not to look suspicious. As they approached the Johnstons', they ducked between houses, grabbing the ladder that Sherman knew Mr Johnston kept there.

Sherman poked his head out to make sure the street was empty before continuing. All was clear.

With his heart racing and his violin case thumping his thigh, he helped Billie carry the ladder across the street and down the block. They snuck it into the Livingstones' backyard, making sure no one was watching. Billie leaned the ladder up against the back of the house beneath Drake's bedroom window.

Sherman nodded at Billie. He crept round to the front of the house.

Sherman took a deep breath and then rang the doorbell. After a minute or two the door swung open and Drake's mother appeared. Her eyes looked sunken and hollow.

All that worry, thought Sherman. *I should tell her the truth. Tell her something to make her feel better.*

It was on the tip of his tongue, but he bit down hard.

Telling her won't bring Drake back. And really, there's not much comfort in the truth anyhow.

"Sherman?" she asked, perking up as she recognized him.

"Hi, *er*...Mrs Livingstone."

Just then Drake's father approached from behind. Sherman coughed loudly giving Billie the signal.

"Sherman, what are you doing here?" asked Mrs Livingstone wearily. Her voice trembled. "You've heard Drake's missing? Have you seen him? Do you know anything?" Her eyes welled with desperation. Hope was clearly fading.

"*Er*, no ma'am," Sherman fumbled. He hated himself.

"Come in Sherman," said Mr Livingstone.

"I, uh, can't stay long," he said stepping inside the doorway. Listening intently, he heard a soft thud. Billie must have been able to pry open the window.

"I, *er*, just came by to ask if, this belongs to you." Sherman held out Stella's pendant. Mrs Livingstone grasped the necklace. When she touched the dark stone Sherman thought he saw her expression lighten. She turned it over in her hands but then her expression darkened again. She shook her head. "Why would you think this belongs to me?" she asked.

Sherman heard another soft thud drift down the stairwell. Mr Livingstone must have heard it too, as his head turned toward the stairs. Sherman's heart froze in his chest.

Quick, say something, anything to get his attention. His line came to him as if out of a dream. "Drake was my best friend—my *only* friend."

Both Mr and Mrs Livingstone's eyes were drawn back toward Sherman. There was a long pause, as an unspoken message passed between them. *I miss him too*, thought Sherman. A tear rolled down Mrs Livingstone's cheek. Sherman was about to say something when he heard another soft thud. *Billie's got to be out.*

"He'll be back," said Sherman quickly. "I don't know how I know, but I just do. He'll be back." Sherman's voice was thick with conviction.

Mrs Livingstone smiled weakly. She handed him the pendant and he tucked it back into his pocket. It felt hot. Like it had been baking in the sun.

* * *

"Tell me again why we stole this old clock," said Billie turning it over in her hands. She gave it a shake. "It rattles like a hunk of junk. I think something's stuck inside it." She shook it again as she boarded the bus and headed for the back. It

87

was already past eight o'clock and they were the only passengers.

"I don't know," said Sherman. "I didn't get a chance to read that far. All I can tell you is Drake got the clock last January for his twelfth birthday. And Stella got this stone pendant."

He extracted the necklace from his pocket and tossed it to Billie who snatched it out of the air.

"Supposedly they were some sort of heirlooms, though his grandma couldn't tell him exactly where they came from. I remember Drake brought the clock along when we went through the light. I don't know anything else about it."

Billie turned the stone over in her hands. "This is really weird."

"What?"

"This stone…it's not a *stone* at all…"

"What do you mean *not a stone?*"

"Stones have crystals…" she held the stone up to the light and examined it carefully. "This hasn't got any."

Sherman thought about this for a moment. "Okay, so it's amorphous."

"*Amorous?*" Billie chuckled. "You mean it's in *love?*"

"Amor-*ph*-ous!" shouted Sherman, his cheeks flushing. "Figures you don't remember our science unit on the earth's crust. Amorphous means no crystals!"

Anger calmed his embarrassment. "It still could be a stone."

Billie tossed the necklace back and Sherman studied it closely.

"Could be obsidian, or opal, or even jet," he said.

Billie shook her head. "René says…"

Sherman rolled his eyes. "I know. I know. Another brother. What's he do? Or dare I ask?"

"GAC."

"Geological Association of Canada?"

"Bingo!"

"No way!" Sherman had had enough. "You are *so* making this up, Billie."

Billie's green eyes sparkled. "Anyway, René says that black opal is really rare—as expensive as diamonds or rubies."

Sherman's jaw dropped. He gave the pendant another examination.

"This isn't a black opal though, Worm. Look. It's got no flashes of red or orange in it."

"Okay, so…"

"And it's not jet either."

Sherman frowned. "How would you know?"

"Too heavy. Jet is fossilized wood. It's really light, you know."

Sherman eyed Billie suspiciously. *How does she know all this stuff? She never gets anything right in class. It's like she's two people... Like Jekyll and Hyde.*

Sherman suddenly suspected there was much more to Wilhelmina Binkleburg than what met the eye.

"Could be obsidian...but doubtful."

"Well, it doesn't matter anyway. The stone and the clock are connected to Stella and Drake. And to the book... And to the eclipse..."

"And what's it all got to do with us?" asked Billie.

"I'm not sure. Not yet."

The bus sped along 14th Avenue and turned north on the Aurora side-road. Its gears screeched to a halt at the end of Sherman's street.

"I'm late," he said, taking the clock from Billie and shoving it into the pocket of his jacket. Billie's pockets were still crammed with something and Sherman resisted the urge to ask what. "My mom's going to have a conniption if I don't turn up soon."

He took a few steps then turned back.

"Thanks, Billie."

Billie grinned. *"Paz dee pro-blame."*

Sherman began walking again, but this time,

he heard her call out from a distance. "Hey Germ! For what it's worth—I believe."

* * *

Shirley Glutz practically pounced on her son as he entered the house. "How was your lesson? What did Ms Wong say? Are you ready to audition for the Philharmonic yet?"

Obviously, she hadn't gotten wind he'd skipped his lesson. Thank goodness for small favors.

"Lesson fine. No audition yet," he replied.

Sherman caught his mother's suspicious frown as he extracted Drake's alarm clock and Stella's pendant from his jacket pocket. He pretended not to notice her inquisitive expression as he headed up the stairs.

"Tired…going to bed," he muttered.

He grimaced and shook his head; he was starting to sound like Billie.

Sherman tossed his violin case, the clock and the pendant onto his bed. He extracted the book from inside the case and crept toward the window. The full moon swam in a sea of stars.

Sherman yawned deeply and then gave his head a shake. Exhaustion was setting in. *No sleep tonight*, he thought. *Don't sleep.*

Sherman sat on the floor cross-legged. He opened the book to the next scene.

Act 2
Scene 6

Sherman Glutz's bedroom.

Sherman Glutz: *(He sits by his window reading a book. He yawns deeply.)* **Four hours left until totality.** *(He yawns again.)* **How will I ever be able to stay awake?** *(He reads aloud.)* **The first time all light in the universe failed, it happened during a solar eclipse. In the exact instant the sun disappeared, Aura had been captured and the world was frozen in darkness. Now, there's going to be a lunar eclipse and I think Umbra is up to his old tricks.** *(He yawns.)* **Only what can I do to stop it with an old clock, a pendant and a magic book?** *(He hears a loud ticking and glances over his shoulder. The full moon in the window of the clock is unusually bright. It's the mirror image of the moon in the sky.)* **How are they connected?** *(He stretches himself across the floor and rests his hands on his folded arms. He yawns deeply one last time and then falls asleep.)*

chapter twelve

An enormous stone tower stretched high into a black sky like a skeletal arm reaching up from a grave. Drake stood motionless on the pedestal, trying hard not to think. Huge columns curled like bony fingers, caging him inside.

He had no idea how long he'd been standing in the highest tower of Umbra's castle—Imwratheer. *Days? Months? Years?* Time didn't seem to matter anymore. He no longer felt hungry or thirsty or tired.

His old clothes were gone. A billowing black garb with an enormous hood cloaked his body and face. He felt strangely exhilarated. A steady beat drummed inside him and he wasn't quite sure if it was the pulsing of his heart or something much more insidious. He was becoming increasingly connected to Umbra. It was as though he and the monster were somehow part of one another.

Inside his head, Drake hummed to keep his brain empty of thoughts. Umbra could read his mind clearer with each passing moment, so he had to be careful not to betray his true intentions. Humming a tune kept his thoughts at bay.

"Stop that infernal racket," said Umbra. "It disturbs me to no end."

"Yes, Shadowmaster."

Drake switched tunes.

"No, no, NO!" said Umbra. "Not another one of your—what do you call them—*Rap* songs?"

"Yes, Shadowmaster. I mean, no, Shadowmaster."

He switched songs again.

"Who is this *Mary*?" demanded Umbra, "And why is she being pursued by a fleecy white lamb?"

Drake couldn't help but smile. "Nothing to worry about, great Shadowmaster."

"Then stop filling my mind with your ridiculous riddles," he bellowed. "We have more important things to think about."

Drake kept humming.

"Spinneret has reached the Obelisk," said Umbra. He extended a long black limb into the distance. "Can you see her? Can you see across our vast dominion and into *hers*?" He pronounced the last word as though it were a curse.

"I see clearly, Shadowmaster," said Drake. "I see across Murk Sea, through Gloom Forest and over Bone Desert. I see into the Bright Side. I see the Obelisk. Its light blinds me even from this distance."

"Good," said Umbra exposing his black pointed teeth. He patted Drake's shoulder with a steely limb. "You are growing in strength, young learner. Soon darkness shall prevail. It shall envelope you along with the universe and you shall see what greatness truly is." He fixed his cold eyes on Drake who felt the prickle of icicles course through his veins. "Provided you do not disappoint me...*again*."

Drake raised his eyebrows. *Hum. Hum. Hum. Hum. Hum, hum, hum...*

He felt Umbra searching his mind. He kept it blank until he was sure the monster was appeased.

"It is all but accomplished," Umbra sighed. "Spinneret will complete the one task I cannot."

Bitterness flowed like venom through his voice. Drake felt the poison surge through his body as well.

"Spinneret will be able to trap the light," he continued. "Aura has surrendered. She has chosen your safety over her own, as was my plan. She will allow herself to be taken, if you are released."

Drake was horrified. He turned toward the dark figure, his eyes full of fear.

"But Shadowmaster..." he pleaded, "I-I don't want to leave your side..."

"Not to worry. She is aware of your treason. She knows you have joined me and yet Aura will sacrifice herself just as long as your safety is insured."

My safety? But...

Drake willed himself not to think.

Hum. Hum. Hum. Hum. Hum, hum, hum...

* * *

Spinneret approaches. He has sent her to capture us.

How can we just let ourselves be trapped and extinguished without so much as a fight?

There are many ways to fight, Stella. Many forms of strength. Patience, my dear Stella, patience.

Yes, but...if Spinneret captures us...we will die. And so will everything that depends on light.

We shan't die quickly. And there is another way. When a hole appears in the sky, the gate will open wide...

A hole in the sky? The gate?
The gate to Eternity...

* * *

Spinneret arrived at the base of the Obelisk with her eight hairy legs the size of small tree trunks. The ancient arachnid clicked her greedy chelicerae as she waited for her prey. Her great jaws, full of powerful muscles, were tipped with venomous fangs. Normally she would paralyze her victim with her venom and then use her scissor-like chelicerae to shred and chop her food. But she would not taste this victim. It was forbidden. She must obey the Shadowmaster and bring the Source of Eternal Light back to him.

As the blinding figure surrendered to her, Spinneret let out a piercing shriek that ripped through the Bright Side. Her eight eyes were stabbed by the force of the light. Her vision was poor at best, only distinguishing between light and shadow, but now she found herself completely sightless.

The huge arachnid cast her silken thread wildly hoping to ensnare her prey. She knew when the sticky coil had struck her target, for she felt the familiar tug. Then she began the arduous task of wrapping and entwining the creature in her thick cable.

Around and around she wove her thread, constructing a tubular silken capsule. A trap. A tomb. And, like a spectacular sunset, slowly all light in the universe began to fade.

chapter thirteen

Tap.

Sherman startled. He was stretched out on the floor.

Tap.

He rubbed his eyes. His mind was soupy. *What happened? What's going on? What's that sound?*

Tap. Tap.

Sherman looked up at the sky and sucked in his breath. The enormous shining disk of the moon was almost gone. The Earth's shadow was swallowing it.

Panic seized Sherman's throat and squeezed. *The eclipse! It's happening! Now!*

Tap.

Something small hit his window. *What is that?* He sprung to his feet and looked into his garden. Standing in the shadows was a dark figure.

Sherman threw open the window. He waved both hands frantically, but it was too late. A small rock sailed through the night air and struck him square in the forehead.

"Billie, you big dummy!" he whispered, clutching his head. "You almost took out my eye!"

"Sorry 'bout that, Klutz," whispered Billie, stifling a giggle.

Sherman had a lot more to say to *The Beast*, but it was best said up close. "Go round the front!" he said motioning wildly.

"Gotcha!" She winked.

Sherman closed the window, dropped the book into the pile on his bed and crept down the stairs. Luckily his parents slept like hibernating bears.

Sherman unlocked the deadbolt and flung open the front door. Billie stood on the porch grinning wildly.

"Hiya…" she began, but Sherman shushed her. He grabbed her by the arm, looked both ways and yanked her inside.

"What are you doing here, Billie? Do you know what time it is?"

"Yup. It's almost *totality*," she whispered. "I thought you'd never wake up."

"Well, you sure fixed that, didn't you?" he snarled, rubbing the growing welt on his forehead. "Why did you come here?" he asked, shaking the remainder of the cobwebs from his brain.

"Two reasons, Butts," she whispered, closing the door behind her. "One, I forgot to give you these." She reached into her jacket pockets and handed him fistfuls of one-and-a-half inch plastic tubes. Sherman looked at them as though they were two-headed dragons.

"What in the *world*—?"

Billie snapped her fingers.

"Light," she said, "Remember, you told me before to bring you some *light*."

Sherman had completely forgotten. When he had asked her to join him in stealing Drake's clock, he had also told her to "bring along some light." He didn't know what it meant when he said it. He eyed the plastic tubes suspiciously. He still wasn't sure.

"And two," said Billie, "we need to get upstairs. It's almost time."

Upstairs? What for? Sherman was more perplexed than ever.

Billie read his confused expression.

"I cheated," she grinned.

"You *what*?"

"I cheated," she said. "I skipped a bunch of pages in that magic book of yours. I read ahead."

Sherman didn't know whether he was furious or jealous or relieved. Leave it to Billie to think up something as simple as skipping ahead. "What do we do now?" he asked.

"We need to get to your clock."

"My clock?"

"Come on," she said, pulling at his sleeve. "It's almost *time*."

Beads of sweat formed on Sherman's upper lip. If some destructive force was going to obliterate the universe, he might be better off letting it happen than risk having his mother wake to find Billie Binkleburg skulking around the house at a quarter after one in the morning. The aftermath in either case would pretty much look the same.

I know I'm going to regret this, he thought.

Still clutching the plastic tubes, he led Billie up the stairs.

As he entered the room, his eyes were immediately drawn to his Moon Phases clock. The plastic tubes fell from his hands. Something was happening. Something very strange. The glowing moon in the sapphire universe of his clock was disappearing exactly like the moon in the sky. And what's more—it was being replaced by a gaping hole. A black hole. And it appeared to be growing.

The clock read 1:16. There was only one minute left until totality.

"Stand still," said Billie. "It's going to happen—*now*."

As the moon outside slipped further into the Earth's shadow, so did its mirror image in the clock. The hole doubled, then tripled in size. In a matter of seconds, the entire face of the clock was gone, leaving an empty chasm surrounded by steel. For a second, Sherman thought he caught a glimpse of something beyond the emptiness—like he was staring into some wacky special effects mirror—and he strained his eyes to make out the image.

His heart stopped beating. He was staring at the back of his own head!

Just then, a blast struck Sherman's ears. It jump-started his heart, wrenching his gaze from the image. A roaring wind tore through the room. Gravity went haywire and everything began to spin. Sherman's feet remained planted firmly on the ground as he circled upside down like he was on some crazy amusement park ride. The ceiling became the floor and then ceiling again. Round and round and round.

"It's a black hole!" cried Billie, her voice barely audible against the eerie moaning of the wind. "We're getting close to the *event horizon*—the point of no return! Hold your breath—it's gonna pull us in!"

Sherman barely had time to take air into his lungs before it was pressed back out. He spun wildly and he felt himself being sucked into the black hole, head first. He opened his mouth to scream, but no sound came out. His body was being stretched like a rubber band, leaving his feet far behind. At the same time, his hands and head were ballooning. He thought they were going to explode. As his insides compressed, thinner, longer, to the point of breakage, he felt like he was being ripped apart.

Then, the last sliver of moon slipped into darkness. Everything went black. The rest of Sherman flew into the abyss like dust into a vacuum.

chapter fourteen

Sherman held his head in both hands. The spinning had stopped, but the dizziness continued. He hated roller-coaster rides and what he had just experienced was a million times worse. In January he had been sucked through light. He recalled the experience vividly now and decided, without question, that being sucked through darkness was a far worse fate.

He stood catching his breath, steadying the rhythm of his thumping heart. The dark was as thick as molasses and the air felt heavy. Breathing was slow and difficult, as though there was barely enough oxygen to fill one lung, let alone two.

Where am I? he wondered. Beneath his feet, the ground hadn't changed. He crouched down and ran his hand along the fibers. *Yup. My bedroom carpet*, he thought. *But...How can that be?* His hand grazed one of the plastic tubes he'd let fall. He gripped it and stood up.

The last time, he had found himself in utter darkness, he had brought along a jar of fireflies. Their flickering glow had been his only solace in a universe swallowed by shadow. Now he had nothing. *Nothing but this stupid plastic tube.* He bit his lower lip and shook his head. "Stupid," he muttered.

"Tsk, tsk," said a distant voice. "No need for insults."

"Billie?" asked Sherman. "Is that you?"

"Sure is," she said. Her voice had a low and vaporous quality, as though sound was moving slower in the dense surroundings. "Where are you?"

"Let's see," he mused. "Other than feeling like my entire body blasted into a zillion atoms that reassembled themselves, hopefully in the right order, I haven't moved a muscle."

"So, what are you waiting for? Use the light I gave you, Mutts," she said.

Sherman rolled his eyes. And yet, Billie's routine insults proved strangely comforting under the circumstances. He heaved a sigh of relief mixed with frustration.

"There's no light, Billie. All you gave me were a bunch of plastic tubes."

"Think again, Worm," said Billie. "Got two words for you—*Mega-Mini Glow-Sticks*."

Glow sticks! Of course! No batteries. No heat. Light by the same principle as fireflies!

Sherman tried to mask his embarrassment at not recognizing the chemical novelty items.

"That's four words, Billie," he huffed.

Sherman knew all about glow sticks, but had never actually held one. He had never been to any wild parties and unfortunately violin concerts were sorely lacking in freaky displays of light.

"Where'd you get all these?" he asked.

"From Ric," she said. Then quickly added, "Brother. DJ."

"Well, your brothers sure cover a wide range of employment, don't they?"

"Drop the sarcasm, Worm, and crack one open, already," she said. Sherman could tell Billie's crocodile grin was plastered ear to ear.

He held the small plastic tube between his fingers. One quick snap and the hydrogen peroxide inside the inner vial mingled with the phenyl oxalate ester and dye solution. Presto! A bright yellow light cut through the darkness and illuminated Sherman's room with a ghostly glow.

"*Kewl!*" said Billie. She picked up another tube and bent it. The light blazed a brilliant blue.

It merged with Sherman's yellow, creating a green aura where the two colors met.

Sherman looked around. Billie appeared normal. Not elongated, bloated or contorted as he'd expected her to be. His bed rested in the same spot, as did his desk, computer and shelf full of music trophies. His violin lay on his bed, and beside it were Drake's clock and Stella's pendant and book. Strewn all over the floor were more of Billie's glow sticks. On the wall above the computer desk was a gaping hole where his clock hung.

It's some kind of a tunnel. Where does it lead? he wondered.

He thought about sticking his hand into the hole, but resisted the urge, keeping a safe distance from it. He was afraid the whole churning and spinning would start all over again.

"Is this awesome, or what?" said a grinning Billie.

"No. Not awesome," said Sherman, shaking his head. "Weird...crazy—check—totally insane!"

"Your room hasn't changed, Butts. Whadya think we should do?"

Billie stood by the window that was completely black. Sherman tried to move his feet but it felt like he was wearing iron shoes.

"Do you mean to tell me, Billie, that you knew

this was going to happen back at the bus stop, and you didn't mention it?"

"Didn't think it was important at the time...we were stealing a clock, remember?"

"Let me try and understand this," said Sherman sucking in air through his clenched teeth. "You found out that gravity would cease to exist in my bedroom, that we'd be sucked—painfully sucked, I might add—through a black hole into some alternate universe for which my clock was some sort of portal. A black hole, Billie, where, in theory, mass has no volume and time stops. And you didn't think any of this was *IMPORTANT ENOUGH TO MENTION*?"

Sherman's voice had risen an octave. He picked up a glow stick and whipped it across the room at Billie. She ducked and it bounced off the window pane.

"Whoa!" she said. "Good arm, Worm. You should try out for the baseball team!"

Sherman glared at her, rage simmering to a boil. Though, in the farthest recesses of his brain, he was secretly thrilled that a super athlete the likes of Billie would place a sport and him in the same sentence.

"Look, let's just go downstairs and find out what's happened."

Sherman moved toward the door. Slowly, he opened it a crack. His spine straightened. The doorknob slid from his grasp and the door creaked open.

There was no landing. No hallway. No stairs. Instead, there was a forest. A pitch-black forest full of enormous white trees.

Sherman stood motionless.

White trees stretched more than fifty feet into a black sky, their leafless branches spreading like cracks in a mirror, their thick roots intertwining along the dark earth like lace. The yellow light of Sherman's glow stick plowed through the darkness, bouncing off the trees and making them glisten.

Sherman shut the door quickly, closed his eyes and took a deep breath. Then he opened the door again. The forest of white trees went on forever.

"I think we've entered the fourth dimension," he whispered.

"Wow," gasped Billie over his shoulder. "I wonder if this is how Dorothy felt."

Sherman snapped to his senses. He couldn't afford to fall apart now.

"So, tell me, Toto, where are we?"

"No idea," said Billie. "No one's ever been sucked into a black hole and returned to tell about it, you know."

"Black holes are in space," scoffed Sherman. "Not bedrooms. Not clocks—space!"

Billie stared blankly.

"They are enormous stars that have burnt out and their entire mass has been squeezed into a single point. Singularity, it's called."

"Well, then, I guess that *singularity* point wound up in your clock," said Billie.

"That's too ridiculous."

"No more ridiculous than what happened to you back in January. And no more ridiculous than what's happened to us now."

Billie had a point. She was one of those annoying people who was an expert at nothing, but knew enough about everything to drive you batty. And in some backward sort of way, she always seemed to make sense. Yup, there was definitely more to her than met the eye.

"You know, Roger says that inside a black hole, time stands still."

"That's all theory," said Sherman, waving his hand dismissively.

"Maybe. But look," she said, pointing to the pile of objects on Sherman's bed, "Drake's clock stopped."

She walked over, picked it up and brought it back to Sherman for a closer look. The hands were

111

still. She shook it and it rattled like something was loose inside. Still, the hands remained motionless.

"Roger also says that according to Einstein's Theory of Relativity, all black holes are connected to each other. That they are like tunnels in the spacetime continuum. You can use them to travel through space and time. Or even link to other universes."

Sherman rolled his eyes.

"I know all about Einstein and his Theory of Relativity, Billie." He would have loved to continue discussing theories of time and space with *The Beast*, only there were more important matters to attend to.

"The thing is, Billie, why are we here? And how do we get home?"

"No clue," said Billie shrugging her shoulders.

"I thought you read ahead in the book?"

"Bits and pieces. Pretty much stopped at the lunar eclipse-black hole part."

Great, thought Sherman, rolling his eyes, *I should have known better than to place my life in the hands of The Beast*.

Billie pushed passed Sherman and took one step outside the room. As her foot grazed the soil, they heard a great sucking noise. The walls of Sherman's bedroom began to shrink.

"It's imploding!" yelled Billie.

"Quick!" shouted Sherman. "Grab what you can!"

Sherman snatched a handful of tubes and shoved them into the pocket of his jeans. He lunged for the book, grappling it and his violin case. The walls caved in on him but he managed to put on his slippers then leap for the door.

Billie scooped up Stella's pendant and a few more glow sticks. She raced for the doorway. It had shrunk to less than three feet tall. She dove out into the strange woods.

Sherman looked back as his bedroom squeezed itself into a tiny ball. It kept on shrinking until it disappeared into itself, leaving nothing behind but a clearing among the ghostly white trees.

Sherman swallowed a dry lump. *Now what?* He stared at the empty spot where his bedroom stood. He took a deep breath and scanned his surroundings. Aside from the huge white trees, there was no sign of vegetation or life. There was a hollow feeling about the place. Quiet and eerie. The air smelled old and stagnant.

"*This is just peachy,*" he sighed, sucking in a musty lungful of dense air. "My bedroom was probably our only way out of this place."

He dropped his violin case and opened Stella's

book. He let out a groan of frustration and cast it aside. "No more full moon means no more words."

"I coulda told you *that*," said Billie, pulling Sherman to his feet.

Sherman stood for moment desperately thinking what to do.

I've lost my crystal ball. What next?

He shuffled closer to one of the white trunks. He ran his hand along its surface. It was as smooth and as hard as bone.

"Take your hand off me," shrieked a voice.

chapter fifteen

Drake stood powerless as all light slowly disappeared from the universe. It began on the Bright Side with a glorious sunset of swirling yellow, orange and crimson, dissolving to violet then fading to black. He looked up from the pedestal that stretched into the vastness of space. Glistening points of distant stars vanished one by one. Galaxies—gone in the blink of an eye.

Then, it was done.

She was captured.

All went black.

Sadness dragged Drake down. He quickly stifled his emotions in the only way he knew how. He repeated a mindless riddle in his head over and over again:

As I was going to St Ives
I met a man with seven wives...

"You are becoming a pest!" roared Umbra. "Can I not enjoy the fruits of my labor in peace without you filling my mind with meaningless dribble?"

"Yes, Shadowmaster. Of course, Shadowmaster."

"Perhaps I should have thought twice when I created the infernal connection that would bind the two of us for all eternity."

"Connection, Shadowmaster?"

That's it. That's how Umbra can read my thoughts. Steal me from my world. Control me.

"Yes, yes and yes," said Umbra.

Drake cupped a hand to his mouth though he hadn't said a word. He had let his thoughts slip. It was a dangerous blunder. He had to be more careful.

"*Er*, tell me, oh great, magnificent Shadowmaster, *exactly* how can poor, insignificant, little me be joined to almighty and powerful you?" he asked.

Umbra sneered. "You are connected to me, in the same way that Aura is joined to your sister, Stella."

Drake squeezed his eyes shut. He couldn't afford to let his thoughts run rampant or he would betray himself. *Stay cool. Stay calm.*

"It was Aura who created the first connection. I merely replicated her move."

Drake was itching to press Umbra for more details. Perhaps if he knew the connection he could undo it. But he couldn't risk thinking. Not now. Not when he was this close.

He willed his mind shut. Every muscle in his body contracted. Sweat trickled down the side of his head. *Don't think. Don't think. Sing something. Quick.*

> *You are my sunshine*
> *My only sunshine...*

Umbra shot him a malevolent look. He was less than amused.

"Oops. Bad choice, huh?" said Drake.

chapter sixteen

Sherman yanked his hand from the tree trunk. "What did you say, Billie?" he asked in a strangled voice. Breathing was difficult. Each lungful took twice the normal effort.

"Huh?"

"You yelled something. I distinctly heard you."

"Nuh-uh. Wasn't me," said Billie flatly, shaking her scraggly mop.

They stared at each other for a moment, before returning their focus to the ghostly white tree. Sherman hesitated. Then he slowly rested his hand on the smooth bark for a second time.

"I said, take your hand off me!"

Sherman startled. He sprang backward, stumbled and fell, landing with a whomp on his behind.

In the mingling light of the glow sticks, Sherman watched as a short creature stepped out of the trunk of the tree as though it were nothing but air. It was less than four feet tall, from the thick mane of wiry matted hair at the top of his head, to the tips of its pointed little shoes. Pure white: White vest. White pants. White body. White face. And white eyes that glistened as they reflected the light of the glow sticks. It resembled a plaster casting of an unpainted garden gnome, though it looked anything but friendly.

It cleared its throat. "Who dares bring light into our world?"

Sherman's jaw dropped. He had seen many frightening creatures on the Halfstone, but that seemed like a lifetime ago.

Panic stole his voice. *Where is the Sherman-osaurus when you need him?*

"*Who*—or should I say *what*—are *you*?" Billie blurted out in her usual aggressive tone.

Sherman wanted to kick her. *For Pete's sake, don't provoke it. Who knows what it's capable of?*

"I should ask you the same!" said the little white man sternly. His voice was high-pitched and squeaky.

"I'm Billie," she said, towering a foot above the figure. She handed Sherman Drake's clock and stuck out her hand as a sign of friendship. Stella's pendant dangled from the gold chain she'd looped around her wrist.

The little gnome gawked at the stone. He took a step back, then did a flip in the air, landing upright.

Billie's eyes narrowed as she spotted his interest in the pendant. She switched it into the hand that held the glow stick. The little man continued to eye the pendant with a mixture of curiosity and delight.

Billie pointed toward Sherman.

"This here's Sherman, but you can call him Worm."

Terrific, thought Sherman. *Now even bizarre otherworldly creatures can feel free to abuse my name.* He gave a half-hearted wave.

"I am Virgil," said the creature, "last of the great White Dwarves." He did another somersault in mid-air, and then fixed them with a penetrating stare. It was tough to see exactly what he was looking at as his eyes were all white with only two beady black dots for pupils. His gaze made Sherman shiver.

At least he said "last", thought Sherman, eyeing the forest of trees and wondering if the rest of the tree trunks had once been inhabited.

"So, are you a good dwarf or a bad one?" asked Billie.

"Not one," said the dwarf sharply. "Neither the other."

It was a cryptic response, but sizing the creature up and down, Sherman decided it was the best they would get.

"Look, Virge, where exactly are we?" asked Billie. "I mean, whadya call this weird place?"

Sherman rolled his eyes and shoved Billie aside. She was doing little to forge a bond of friendship between herself and the dwarf.

She shoved him back, then snatched Drake's clock.

"Mr Virgil, sir," he began, rising to his feet. "I must apologize for the rude behavior of my *friend*." He shot Billie a *stop-talking-now* look. Then he gave the dwarf a reverent bow.

"We really don't mean to disturb you. We've come here by accident. We seem to be lost."

The dwarf's expression softened a bit. When he spoke again his voice had lost most of its hostility.

"You are in Limbo Forest," he said, stretching his arms out toward the network of trees. "The forest surrounds the Pit of Eternity."

"The Pit of Eternity!" shouted Billie. "This is getting cooler by the second."

Sherman blasted her with another *will-you-shut-up-already* look. Billie responded with a crooked flash of her braces. Sherman paused for a moment to think.

"Is there a way out of here?" he asked.

The white dwarf searched Sherman's face. Was he looking for courage? Malice? Or something entirely different?

"There is no way out of Limbo Forest except, perhaps, through the Pit of Eternity. The pit spirals downward in circles and I have seen but as far as the Fourth Ring. *If* there is an exit, it lies deeper." Sherman and Billie exchanged curious glances.

The dwarf continued, his eyes tapering suspiciously. "If you have not been here before," he said pointing to the pendant dangling from Billie's wrist, "how is it you have come to be in possession of a *Spirit Stone?*"

"A *what?*" asked Billie, looking down at the pendant dangling from her wrist.

"Did you say a *Spirit Stone?*" Sherman reached for Stella's pendant, but Billie yanked it back.

She punched Sherman in the arm. "Told you it wasn't obsidian!" she said smugly.

"Can we please save this argument for another time?" said Sherman through clenched teeth.

He turned to face Virgil and smiled. "What

exactly is a *Spirit Stone?*"

The dwarf glared at Sherman. "It has been reported to me that the Sixth Ring of the Pit of Eternity is the location of The Gorge," Virgil said. "Each living creature has a Spirit Stone. The stone shelters their essence. It contains their source of energy and power. The stones lie in The Gorge, in safety, for all eternity."

"Whoa!" said Billie. "You mean I got one of these things too?" She swung the pendant around her index finger. It spun out of control, slipped off her finger and conked Sherman on the head. It dropped to the ground with a *thunk*.

"Well, Billie, he did say *each living creature* and you certainly are a *creature*," snapped Sherman, rubbing the side of his head. "And I suppose we're still *alive*, though it somehow doesn't feel much like it anymore..."

"Careful, Worm," smiled Billie. "Don't go jinxing us, or anything."

Billie had a different smile for every occasion. This smile seemed to say: "We're doomed."

Sherman surveyed the white trees stretching high into what looked like empty space. He was thinking the same thing.

Before either Billie or Sherman could stop him, Virgil picked up the pendant. The black stone looked like a hole in the palm of his white hand. "This is not an entire Spirit Stone," he said, analyzing the pendant. "Spirit Stones are much larger. This is but a portion. Though, I must say, I have never heard of a Spirit Stone being split before. It must have been extracted by ancient and powerful magic."

Ancient. Powerful. Sherman nodded. *Been there. Done that.*

Then suddenly it was as though someone threw a switch in his brain, illuminating a thought that until now lay in darkness. "If it's only a piece of a Spirit Stone," he said, "then that must be why we're here."

Billie scrunched up her face. Then her eyebrows shot up. "You're right!"

"I have no idea how this will bring light back to our universe, but we need to put the missing piece back where it belongs," said Sherman. He reached for the stone, but Virgil closed his hand on the pendant and it disappeared in his white fist.

"You may have your stone," he said in a menacing tone, "but only if you give me something in exchange."

"Why you little pixie!" shouted Billie. She lunged for the pendant, her glow stick dropping to the ground. The dwarf stepped back inside his tree and Billie smashed into it with a whomping thud.

"Hey!" she yelled rubbing her head. "Get back out here, you thieving troll!"

"*Dwarf!*" shouted Virgil from the safety of his dwelling. "*Dwarf—not troll!*"

"Whatever!" Billie pounded her fists against the solid trunk, but it was no use. It was as though the dwarf had become one with the tree.

"If I had Reggie's chainsaw, you'd be in big trouble little elf. Big trouble!"

"Reggie?" mouthed Sherman.

"CILA," she mouthed back. "Canadian Inter-collegiate Lumberjacking Association."

Sherman sighed. *I can't keep all these brothers straight.*

"Dwarf!" shouted Virgil angrily. "Dwarf!"

Sherman grabbed hold of Billie's waist and dragged her away, cussing and thrashing. Under different circumstances, it would have been a ridiculous sight.

"We'll get the stone back," he said calmly. "Let's just promise to help the dwarf."

"Why should we help him?" asked Billie. "What's he ever done for us?"

"I will take you through to the Fourth Circle," said Virgil. "You will need a guide. And I can take you there."

Billie stopped kicking at the tree and bent down to pick up her blue glow stick.

"Through the Fourth Circle? You've got a deal," said Sherman without conferring with her.

"I have your word?" asked Virgil.

"You have our word," he said. "Now come back out of your tree and tell us what you want us to do."

chapter seventeen

Virgil reappeared out of the trunk. He held the stone pendant out to Sherman, but Billie sprang between them and snatched it. She opened the clasp and swung the gold chain-link around her neck.

She patted the stone, eyeing the white dwarf haughtily. "Safe keepings."

Billie wearing a necklace? thought Sherman. *Now I know I'm in an alternate universe!* He shook his head in disbelief.

"Okay," he said to Virgil, "the deal is you see us safely through the Fourth Circle in exchange for our help. So, what exactly do you want us to do?"

Virgil leapt into the air and clicked his heels. He let out a creepy giggle.

"I will guide you, but your safety is not guaranteed." His lips parted exposing a crown of pointed white teeth. "There are perils in each circle. If you overcome these obstacles it will be by your own strength and prowess, not mine."

"We can't trust that sneaky gnome!" snarled Billie, moving toward him with one balled fist. "I'll show you strength and prowess all right!"

Virgil ducked behind Sherman.

"*Dwarf!*" he squeaked, stomping his foot. "I am a *dwarf!*"

Sherman held Billie back by her shoulders.

"Stop it, both of you!" he ordered. "Just tell us what you want, Virgil."

"One promise," he said slyly. "One promise to do *as* I ask, *when* I ask it."

"I'm not promising anything, you little leprechaun, unless I know exactly what I'm promising," said Billie. She grabbed Sherman by his sweatshirt and pulled him aside.

"Come on, Worm," she whispered. "We've got the pendant, let's just take off."

"Take off *where*, Billie?" said Sherman in a hushed voice. "First of all, we've already made a promise, and I, for one, stand by my word."

Billie rolled her eyes. "*Promise Shmomise!*"

"Second, since there's no full moon around, the magic diary no longer works, so we have no idea where to go and what dangers lie ahead. That dwarf over there does." He motioned his chin toward Virgil who twitched, hopping from foot to foot. "Like it or not, we need that guy as much— if not more—than he needs us."

Sherman left Billie standing off to the side and returned to face Virgil. "I promise," he said holding out his hand as a symbol of his pledge.

The white dwarf paused for a moment, and then shook on it, sealing the deal. Virgil's hand felt cold and leathery. Sherman cringed.

"And that one?" asked Virgil pointing toward Billie. "She must promise as well."

"Give him your word, Billie," said Sherman.

"Fine," she said, "but don't expect me to shake his scrawny white hand or nothing."

"Done," said Sherman. "Now, where do we begin?"

Virgil twirled in the air. "Follow me," he said, and then skipped off. He wove through the maze of chalky trunks, snorting and laughing as he jigged along.

"Hey!" shouted Sherman. "Wait up!" He snatched his violin case and quickly tucked Stella's book inside. He shuffled after Virgil in his brown, corduroy slippers.

Holding Drake's clock and her glow stick, Billie brought up the rear.

For what felt like hours, the two scrambled along a few paces behind the white dwarf. He glided effortlessly between, around and *through* trees, laughing and chuckling to himself merrily. Sherman stepped gingerly over the interlaced roots, periodically glancing upward into the ceiling of twisted branches that made the black sky appear like a dome of cracked glass. Tree trunk after tree trunk, the landscape stayed the same.

"Are you sure you're not leading us in circles, pixie?" yelled Billie.

"*Dwarf!*" snarled Virgil. "And *yes*, we are traveling in circles." He squealed like a pig. "Limbo Forest is one giant circle, with no beginning and no end."

"So where are we going?" asked Billie.

"You shall soon see," he smirked.

Billie eyed Sherman.

"Sure hope you know what you're getting us into, Squirmy."

Sherman offered a thin grin. *Sure hope so too*, he thought.

The glow sticks were surprisingly bright, cutting through the darkness like tiny floodlights. Sherman could see far ahead. He noticed they were approaching a gap in the trees. Virgil broke through the last tree trunk and stopped short. Sherman reached the spot and froze. They were standing on the edge of an enormous black pit the size of a lake. Gripping his violin case in one hand, Sherman extended his glow stick over the rim, but even the bright light couldn't penetrate the darkness.

Billie barreled up from behind. She nearly fell over the edge but grabbed onto Sherman in the last second. The two teetered on the brink before falling backwards, landing in the dirt.

Sherman's glow stick slipped through his fingers and sailed through the air, plummeting down into the pit. It illuminated bits and pieces of the cavity before disappearing into its dismal depths.

"Yikes!" yelled Billie, ruffling Sherman's hair. "Almost lost you there, Germ."

"Are you *trying* to kill us, Billie?" huffed Sherman, shoving her aside and springing to his feet. He reached into his pocket and cracked open a new glow stick. As the hydrogen peroxide mingled with the dye solution a piercing green light filtered through the air.

"Now that you have become somewhat acquainted with the Pit of Eternity," said Virgil, "let us enter."

He led them to a spot on the rim of the chasm.

A square slab of rock lay flat in the black earth. It was about four feet by four feet and was slick and polished like marble or granite. It reminded Sherman of a gravestone.

The green light illuminated an inscription carved into the stone in an undecipherable language.

Virgil read the inscription: "*Abandon hope*."

Sherman swallowed hard.

"Not exactly a welcome mat." He tried to chuckle but the sound died back into his throat and he coughed.

"Well, what do you think, Billie?"

"Got news for you, Germ," she said in an uncharacteristically soft voice, "I abandoned all hope ages ago."

Sherman heard a low groan and the scraping of stone grinding against stone. He gritted his teeth as the flat rock lifted like a trap door. It exposed a narrow staircase of crumbling rock.

"After you!" said Billie, bowing mockingly to the dwarf. Virgil scowled in return.

The stone steps spiraled downward through a tunnel of thick black earth. Virgil moved quickly, but Sherman and Billie stood locked in a silent stare that begged the question: *Who goes first?* Billie finally shrugged and began curling her way downward. Sherman followed gingerly, making certain one foot was sure before stepping down with the other.

As he descended, Sherman noticed bits and pieces of white tree roots sewn through the soil. He accidentally brushed up against the wall. It crumbled easily and showered him with dirt.

The steps beneath him were narrow and difficult to navigate. He stole a glance behind him, but the trap door was no longer visible. Fear, the size of a boulder, stuck in his throat.

"Two hundred and sixty-seven...two hundred and sixty-eight..."

Sherman could hear Billie's voice counting the steps grow faint. He picked up the pace, slipping only once. He landed on his behind and slid down a few steps before righting himself and carrying on.

"Five hundred and eighty-nine steps," said Billie as Sherman reached the bottom. There, an archway opened up into a hollow chamber of rock. It was a cave of some sort, complete with stalagmites and stalactites rising and descending from floor to ceiling.

"You okay, Vermin?" asked Billie, slapping bits of dirt from Sherman's shoulder.

"Fine," he said, shoving her hand away. "And stop touching me already!"

They moved toward Virgil who stood like a

statue at the mouth of the cave. Beyond him they saw what looked like a lush field of green grass and wild flowers swaying in the breeze.

"You stand on the cusp of the First Circle," said Virgil. "Do you still wish to continue?"

Nothing beyond the cave appeared menacing. It was a lovely field. In the light of the green and blue glow sticks, it appeared like the twilight of a beautiful spring day.

"Outta my way, dwarf!" said Billie, pushing past Virgil.

Sherman followed Billie into the field. He inhaled deeply. The air was fresher and lighter here—easier to digest. A pleasant scent like the aroma of his mother's favorite herbal teas filled his nostrils. Jasmine. Elderflower. Rosehips. Camomile.

Sherman's mind began to drift. *Sunny days. Lazy afternoons. Sipping lemonade from a curly straw, sitting in my backyard in mom's Adirondack chair. Bird chirping happily. Clouds drifting by...*

"The First Circle is known as the Circle of Sloth." Virgil's words shook Sherman from his trance.

"Sloth, you say?" Billie chuckled. She waved a dismissive hand. "Come on Squirmy. Even you could outrun those lazy monkeys." She marched forward stepping into the meadow, plowing through the flowers and lush green grass.

"There are no creatures here except *you*," said Virgil. "And nothing to outrun but yourselves."

"Are you gonna guide us, or what, *brownie?*" she called over her shoulder ignoring his riddle.

"As you wish." Virgil humphed and then scuttled to take the lead once again.

As they walked though the lush green fields brimming with daisies and poppies and sweet grass, Sherman began to feel giddy. He chuckled a few times to himself, without knowing why.

"What's so funny, Germ?" Billie smiled, unable to stop herself from laughing as well.

Sherman felt a sudden surge of rapture. His mind clouded with dreamy thoughts. *Why am I here again? What am I supposed to do?* The answer was distant. The smells, sights and sounds were pushing his purpose farther and farther into a foggy haze. The air was intoxicating. He was drunk with happiness. Each breath made his head feel lighter and dizzier. He suddenly felt compelled to plop himself down and roll in the grass. He released his violin case and stretched out onto the ground. It was like velvet and marsh-mallows and fluffy cotton balls.

"Hey Billie," he called. "You've got to try this!"

Billie turned back and laughed at Sherman. She fell to the ground and began to roll unable to control her giggles.

Sherman's eyelids grew heavy. Drowsiness overcame him. Everything was so beautiful. So pleasant. So blissful. He could just lay here forever. *Forever. Forever...*

"I see you both are susceptible to the influence of Sloth," grinned Virgil. "I would just as soon leave you here to blissfully rot, but I do need you to fulfill that promise you made." He reached over and flicked Sherman's ear.

"Hey!" said Sherman, but Virgil flicked him again, this time harder. He swatted Billie in the face with a huge bunch of daisies.

"Get lost, creepy gnome!" she said. Anger forced her brain to emerge from its haze.

Sleepy and lethargic, Sherman dragged himself to his sluggish feet. He fought desperately against the powerful desire to lie down and rest. He knew if he lay again in the sweet smelling grass he would never have the energy to get up.

He forced thoughts of sleep and dreams out of his mind. *Think of Drake. Think of Stella. Think of the universe and the light. Think of school. The violin. Mom.*

That's it. Mother. Sherman knew thoughts of her would keep sloth at bay.

His legs felt like tree trunks as he trudged along. His jelly-filled knees nearly gave out more than once.

"Not much further," said Virgil. "We are almost there."

Sherman willed himself to keep moving until finally, he could go no further. He collapsed to the ground.

He was at the top of a sharp incline. His body fell hard jarring the glow stick loose from his grip. Hugging his violin case, he began to roll down the steep slope. Wild thoughts spun inside his brain. *Never get out. Stay here forever.* Downward he tumbled, until his body bumped along what felt like gravel beneath him. He jolted to his senses and snapped to attention.

"Ouch! Hey!" he shouted, coming to an abrupt stop at the bottom of the hill. His violin case made it through with only nicks in the leather casing, but Sherman's arms were scraped and bruised. Billie lay not far away, still clutching her blue glow stick and Drake's clock.

"Congratulations," said Virgil. "You have made it through the Circle of Sloth. Now enter the Second Circle, better known as the Ring of Walls."

chapter eighteen

Umbra stretched two long bony limbs toward the black sky as absolute darkness rained down on him.

"It is done!" he said, hissing like a snake. The hood fell from his head revealing for the first time white hair streaming from a black skull, pulsing with veins. "The Shadowmaster has triumphed. I now reign supreme!"

You are nuts, thought Drake.

Umbra flashed his crooked teeth.

"What was that?"

"Oh, er," Drake caught himself. "I'd love some nuts!"

"You dare mock me?"

"Of course not, great Shadowmaster," said Drake quickly. "I worship you. I revere you. I stand in awe of your very being..."

"Enough!" said Umbra holding up his hand. "Even your accolades begin to annoy me."

As they spoke Spinneret approached in silence. First one leg, then another, until out of the tower doorway emerged a huge hairy spider the size of a bulldozer. It towed an enormous silken capsule.

"Finally, she arrives," said Umbra coldly. "Come, Drake. Let us have one final visit with your sister before she passes into infinity and takes Aura and the light with her."

Umbra touched the sticky tube.

Spinneret withdrew, her greedy chelicerae searching the darkness for food. The spider came within a hair's breath of Drake, who closed his eyes and trembled, expecting to become the arachnid's next snack.

"Off with you, Spinneret!" said Umbra. "Your task is complete. Other delicacies await you in your lair."

Drake heaved a sigh of relief as the monstrous hairy spider scuttled backwards. She cast her silk over the side of the tower and with a great leap disappeared downward.

Umbra turned his black skull toward the silken capsule.

"No tricks will save you this time, Aura," he said. "You have miscalculated, I am afraid. You have housed the last remnant of your great spirit inside this weak shell of the creature called Stella.

I need only destroy her, and you will perish along with her."

Out of the folds of his billowing black cloak, Umbra drew a great sword. It seemed to be forged of the same black metallic stone that made up his castle.

In one swift movement, he extended the weapon to Drake.

"Prove your devotion to me once and for all. Smite the weak. Destroy all light forever."

Drake's heart beat out of control.

chapter nineteen

Sherman snapped open a new glow stick. Red light sliced through the darkness.

Before him lay a narrow gravel road. It was carved out of great jutting rock that rose straight up on either side. As he moved forward with cautious steps, Sherman felt as though he were entering a triangular tunnel of shale and limestone.

The path twisted and turned on a low grade. As Sherman shuffled along in his slippers, he couldn't shake the sensation that he was descending slowly through the bowels of a monster.

Though Virgil skipped merrily along, singing, "Follow the gravely road, Follow the gravely road," and Billie kept whispering in his ear through clenched teeth, "Can I kill him now? How about *now?* Now?", Sherman couldn't squelch the feeling that something treacherous lay ahead.

They rounded a particularly sharp corner. Sherman saw a wall looming in the distance. It appeared to bar the path.

As he trudged along Sherman was filled with trepidation, but as he drew nearer he sighed with relief.

The wall was no more than eight feet high. There were footholds etched into the surface that would make it easy to climb.

"*That's* the big challenge?" scoffed Billie. "I can climb that stone wall blindfolded with one arm tied behind my back."

"Perhaps," said Virgil. "If it *were* a wall of *stone*."

He clapped his little hands and did three quick leaps.

"You see it is not a *wall of stone* at all, but rather, a *wall of fear* that you and your friend must attempt."

Sherman had a sinking feeling in the pit of his stomach. He knew Billie's boasting was premature.

"Wall of fear?" Sherman asked, but before the words had completely left his lips, he saw the stone transform before his eyes into a slithering, hissing wall of snakes. He gasped and sprang backward. He clutched his violin case to his chest for protection.

"S-snakes!" he shouted, his knees wobbling. "It's covered in s-snakes!"

"Not snakes," yelled Billie from behind him. "Scorpions!"

"I th-think I kn-know s-snakes when I see them!" stuttered Sherman.

"They're scorpions, I tell you!" insisted Billie. "And there must be ten million of 'em!"

Virgil did a pirouette. He laughed aloud.

"One is right and so is the other," he sang. "Your fears are not the same, so why should the wall be the same?"

"That little ogre is really getting on my nerves, Squirmy," said Billie, shooting daggers at Virgil with her eyes. "If that's the truth, then tell me, Virge, what are you afraid of? What does the wall look like to you?"

Virgil shook his head. "Not going to tell. Won't say a word."

"All right then. Come on Worm," said Billie lowering her chin in determination. "This is going to be easy."

"How do you figure?" said Sherman unable to peel his eyes off the writhing wall of pythons, cobras, boas and vipers.

"We see different things, right?" asked Billie. "So that must mean neither of them are really there."

Billie's unique brand of logic always brought Sherman's sense of reason to a standstill.

"Okay, Worm," she said, "You go ahead..."

"What?" yelled Sherman, anger wrenching his gaze from the hissing reptiles. "Why *me*? Why not *you*?"

"Because..." said Billie. "I'm a better thrower."

"Oh, that makes *loads* of sense!" said Sherman sarcastically.

"Listen, you go first, then I toss over the violin case and the clock and the glow sticks. You catch them from the other side."

"You said I was a good thrower too, that I should even try out for the baseball team. Why can't *you* go first and *I* throw?"

"Germ, you're wearing slippers. If you fall, who will be here to catch you?"

"I hate you, Billie..." he said as she pushed him forward. She pried the glow stick and the violin case from his death-grip.

Sherman closed his eyes and took a deep breath.

The Shermanosaurus knows no fear. The Shermanosaurus can leap over this wall in a single bound. The Shermanosaurus...hates snakes!!!!

Sherman reached out a trembling hand. With his eyes still sealed, he inched forward until his fingertips grazed something solid. *The wall!* He sighed.

"I can feel it, and it feels just like stone!" he called out to Billie.

The hissing sound was all around him. He placed another shaking hand on the wall, feeling around for a notch to grab hold of. His foot found one of the holes. Slowly, Sherman heaved his weight up. He swallowed hard as he left the ground.

After several more tentative moves, he gained enough confidence to open his eyes. He nearly pushed off of the wall when he saw his hands smothered in slimy reptilian bodies.

"AHHH!" he screamed, shutting his eyes. Once again, he felt nothing but wall.

"Don't give up now, Vermin!" called Billie from behind. "You're almost at the top. Just a little bit further."

Sherman willed himself not to think of what he'd seen. He had to focus on what he felt—which was nothing but stone.

Finally, his hand pressed flat on the top. He pulled himself up so that he was straddling the wall. Then, gingerly, he lowered himself down the other side.

He was elated.

"I did it!" he yelled when his feet hit the ground. An enormous sense of pride filled his chest.

No sooner had he made it over then a glow stick sailed over the wall. It struck him in the eye. "Ouch! Couldn't you at least give me some kind of warning, Billie?" he shouted.

"Heads up!" yelled Billie.

Sherman had just enough time to stretch out his hands before his violin came hurling over the wall. He caught the precious instrument and sighed with relief. Then Drake's clock came crashing down. It landed on his foot.

"One of these days, Billie...one of these days..."

Billie scaled the wall fairly quickly. Virgil followed. The trio set off once again down the gravel path. There were more walls to conquer.

After the scorpions, Billie braved tarantulas, shark jaws, giant squids, killer bees and orthodontists.

At the fifth wall, she couldn't help but laugh out loud. "Tomatoes?" she snorted. "What's up with that?"

"Yes. Tomatoes, Billie." Sherman refused to look her in the eye. "I can't stand the texture, if it's any business of yours. All that skin and seeds," he began to retch. "And they smell funny.

And they're slimy…"

"Okay, okay," said Billie shaking her head. "I get the picture. Just move quicker already. Or do I have to chase you with a bottle of ketchup?"

At the sixth wall, she stopped again while Sherman explained about the wraithworms he'd come across on his last journey with Stella and Drake.

"Two-headed gelatinous worms the size of fire hoses?"

"You had to be there," said Sherman, doing his best to climb quickly without opening his eyes. He made his way safely to the other side.

Sherman had begun to think the Ring of Walls was getting easier, when he came to an abrupt standstill in front of the seventh and final wall. In front of him, the great wall of stone quickly morphed into an abyss of darkness. Even the glow stick's light could not penetrate it.

He swallowed hard as he came to grips with his ultimate fear: that Umbra had once again captured Aura and, if Sherman failed, the universe would remain dark forever.

His hands quivered as he extended them into the black void of the wall and they disappeared up to his elbows. He could feel the wall, but he'd lost his hands.

Beads of sweat formed on his upper lip. He tried desperately to talk himself out of the fear.

You can do it. You are the Shermanosaurus. You will replace the Spirit Stone in time and save the universe from Umbra's darkness.

A new sense of urgency pressed him forward. At the same time a weird sense of calm steadied his nerves and he actually began to believe he'd succeed in his quest. He breathed deeply as he began to scale his last, greatest fear.

Sherman was half way over a wall, when he heard Billie gasp. He turned to see Billie standing facing the wall with a stone-cold stare. She appeared to have turned three shades of pale.

"What is it?" whispered Sherman. "What do you see?"

She didn't move, but continued to stare wide-eyed at the wall.

"Billie?"

"I can't do it," she said softly. "Not this one, Germ."

"Come on," he coaxed. "Whatever it is, it can't be as bad as all that."

Billie closed her eyes then opened them again. She shook her head.

"If you don't tell me what it is, I can't help you," said Sherman. "Remember Billie, you said it yourself, this isn't real."

She shook her head again. "This one is."

"Come on, Billie. Tell me and I can help you."

Her lips parted slightly, and one small word slipped through the gap: "Failure," she whispered, her whole body slumping.

"Failure?" said Sherman.

"All my report cards, all my tests, all my homework, everything I've ever blown...Words out of order, math problems I couldn't solve, projects I've failed...it's all up there, Worm, staring me down."

Sherman couldn't understand it. Any school work he'd ever failed had been by choice. He could choose to do well or choose to do poorly. And what's more, he didn't care either way. He didn't understand this fear. How could the fear of failure be so paralyzing?

"Billie," he said, as the darkness in front of him seamed suddenly meaningless, "tell me what you see and I will help you through."

Billie took a deep breath and put one hand up to the wall. "It's a math problem," she said sadly. "12 x 48 ÷ (4 x 3) + 4? = ," she read with a shaky voice.

"That's easy," said Sherman. "It's only order of operations. Just remember BEDMAS—brackets, exponents, division, multiplication, addition and subtraction. Now look at the problem again. The brackets say 4 x 3 which is 12. Now do the exponent, 4 to the power of 2 is 4 x 4 which is 16. Now the division. 48 divided by 12 is 4. So, 12 x 4 + 16 is 64. There you go. Easy as pie!"

"That's all easy for you, Worm," sighed Billie. "But when I try to think, sometimes my mind just goes blank and then things dance around doing back flips on the page all out of order. I see things and I know what they mean, know what I want to say, but it gets jumbled in my brain."

Sherman was starting to wonder about Billie. Who was this big bully who knew so much and so little at the same time, who claimed to have twelve brothers, who made logical sense out of a tangled mess, but couldn't think straight enough to answer a simple math problem?

"It's all in your head, Billie. Success. Failure. It's nothing but a state of mind. Like that wall in front of you. It isn't real."

Billie stopped and thought about this for a second. She looked up and stared long and hard at Sherman's encouraging smile. When she moved next, a scowl of determination illuminated her face.

She tackled the wall with slow but steady movements. Sherman helped her with each math equation, each history question, each word definition, each scientific conclusion. Together they solved the problems one by one until she reached the top.

As they sat together on the top of the wall, Sherman saw something new in Billie's eyes. If he wasn't mistaken, it was something like pride.

They both landed with a thud on the other side.

"Thanks, Sherman," she said.

It was the first time she'd called him by his name.

As they followed Virgil along the remainder of the gravel path, they walked slower, side by side.

"I don't get you, Billie," said Sherman. "On one hand you act like you're dumb. But you know things—I know you do. So why don't you do well in school? What's the big mystery?" he asked.

She sighed heavily, regaining her usual tough exterior. "I'm what they call *Gifted—Learning Disability—behavioral*."

"The behavior part I get," said Sherman, rolling his eyes as fleeting images of Billie punching his arm, ruffling his hair, and bouncing balls off his head flashed through his mind. "But Gifted? *You* are *gifted*?" He puzzled for a moment. "How can you be Gifted and Learning Disabled at the same time?"

"You just can," shrugged Billie. "It's like it's all in there, and then some." She pointed to her head.

"But the information has trouble getting out."

Sherman furrowed his brow trying to wrap his mind around the concept.

"Doesn't matter though," she continued. "Kids all just treat me like I'm some kinda dumb animal, right? Who cares that I know stuff? All that counts are tests and report cards, right? If you don't do well on them, you're just a dumb beast, right?"

Sherman cast his eyes downward. He felt his ears burning with shame. How could he ever have thought of Billie as *The Beast?* That was mean. Cruel. And he, if anyone, should understand what it's like to be different.

For the first time, his heart softened toward Billie. She was, after all, kind of like him.

As she tossed her head back, he noticed the gold necklace glisten around her neck.

There was something different about her. Sherman quickly shrugged off the feeling.

"Hey Billie," he asked, "do you really have all those brothers, or did you just make them up to hide your gifted side?"

Billie smiled and her braces glistened in the glow stick light.

The gravel path abruptly ended. Virgil, who had been skipping along several paces ahead, stopped at the edge of a steep precipice.

"We have passed the Second Circle." He pointed to steps carved into the face of the rock. "Down there is the Third Circle through which flows the River of Woe."

chapter twenty

Sherman held his glow stick over the edge. Narrow steps descended steeply down a rocky crag disappearing into darkness.

With nothing to grab hold of should he lose his balance, Sherman wondered for a second if he'd do better sliding down on his behind.

"Here Billie," he said stooping to pull off his slippers and socks. "Shove these in your pockets, will you?"

"No way!" she snapped, slapping his hand aside.

"Look, I'm not going down *that*, in *these*," he said pointing to the sharply descending steps. "Bare feet will give me a better grip."

"How is it I end up having to pocket your fungus-filled footwear?"

"*You* have a jacket with deep pockets," he pointed out. "*I*, on the other hand, am wearing nothing but jeans and a sweatshirt. Need I remind you that my room imploded before I could gather proper Black Hole attire? And since you didn't even have the decency to warn me—here you go."

He thrust the sweaty slippers into her hands. She accepted them begrudgingly.

"Why are we still carrying all this junk?" asked Billie, shaking Drake's rattling clock and pointing to Sherman's violin case.

"Junk? It's a *Stradivarius*," he said incredulously, but her expression remained blank.

"It's worth a fortune, Billie. My mom would skin me alive and feed me to wolves if I let this violin out of my sight," he sighed. "And as for Drake's clock, I'm not sure. But we had to risk stealing it, so it must be important."

"Whatever you say, Germinator," said Billie.

That's a new one, thought Sherman. *Almost like it better than Shermanosaurus.*

He decided it would be best not to tell her.

"Quickly," chided Virgil, clucking his tongue. "We shall have to summon the ferryman. Unless, of course, you prefer to *swim*." He chortled as though the last word was some sort of secret joke.

An uneasy feeling settled in Sherman's stomach once again.

"I don't trust that dwarf," muttered Billie

shaking her head. "He's got something up that little white sleeve of his."

"Maybe," said Sherman, "but there's nothing we can do right now except follow him."

With calculated steps, they descended the cliff, lower and lower toward a darkening mass. Sherman could hear a rush of water. A foul stench rose like a cloud around him. With each step, the odor grew more rank. It was as though they were approaching a sewage plant.

"What *is* that smell?" asked Billie.

"That," said Virgil, "is the River of Woe. What you smell is all the waste of the universe. This river is where all evil energy is cleansed, leaving behind the brine of malevolence, cruelty and spite."

"Not exactly the kind of river you'd want to fish in," said Sherman glumly.

Billie forced a grin. "Sure makes your socks smell like roses in comparison." She tucked Drake's clock under one arm and pinched her nose.

The closer they came to the bottom of the cliff, the more repugnant the air grew and the louder the water roared. As they reached the last step, they found themselves standing on the rocky banks of a raging river. It seemed to gush out of the mountainside, flow straight for a while and then curve sharply. A vaporous mist hung above the water so that they were unable to see across to the other side.

"The water looks red." Sherman squinted. "Must be this light."

"It is not your light that makes the river appear red," said Virgil. "The River of Woe is a stream of boiling blood."

"That is just nasty!" said Billie. "No way I'm crossing that!"

"Choose what you will," said Virgil. "Return whence you came and roam Limbo Forest with me for all eternity."

"Some choice," she said, scowling at the dwarf. "I think I'll take my chances in the boiling blood. So, where's this ferryman-dude?"

"Call the ferryman by name and he will come," said Virgil.

"Okay, what's his name?" asked Sherman.

"It begins with PH and ends with YAS, and in the middle you find LE and G."

Billie tried to clasp a hand on Sherman's mouth, but she was too late.

"Phlegyas," said Sherman, pushing Billie's hand away. "Why didn't you just say it?"

"Because," said Virgil stifling a giggle, "he who calls the ferryman is responsible for the fare."

"Do you believe me now, Germ?" said Billie.

"You can't trust this dwarf farther than you can throw him...speaking of which..." She moved closer to Virgil. "How about I toss him into the boiling blood right now?"

Just then, the ghostly sound of a foghorn echoed in the distance. A black barge emerged from the wall of mist. A lone cloaked figure steered the vessel with a long wooden pole that it held in skeletal hands. The ferry glided toward them as though the waters were still.

Sherman sucked in his breath as the barge approached. He had the distinct impression that the figure steering the vessel was not of the living.

"You called?" said a raspy voice.

"Quickly," said Virgil. "We must board at once."

"What about the fare?" asked Sherman cautiously.

"Pay the ferryman once you arrive at the other side," said Virgil.

"Don't trust him!" said Billie. "It's some kind of trick."

Sherman had a sinking feeling. He knew Billie was right; the dwarf was hiding something. Still, there was no turning back now. He had to think of Drake, of Stella and of the light. The Spirit Stone was the key and no matter what it took, he would return the stone to where it belonged.

"We have to trust him, Billie," sighed Sherman. "We have no other choice. We can't turn around."

He stepped aboard the rickety boat.

Virgil hopped aboard the barge and Billie reluctantly followed. She took a seat on the shaky wooden planks that were charred and black as coal.

As the ferryman steered the barge away from the shore, they were sucked into the powerful current. They zipped off at tremendous speed.

"Where are we going?" shouted Sherman, his voice sounding weak over the bubbling rapids.

"The river spirals downward, completing seven circles before rushing over a waterfall past the City of Nix. No need to worry though, we exit before the drop. The road there will take us to the Palace of Al."

The city of what? The palace of who? Questions filled Sherman's head, but he knew his voice would be lost behind the roar of the rapids. He found himself clinging to the side of the barge with both hands as it swirled and curled its way downstream through the thick curtain of fog.

They completed circle after circle, rushing faster and faster and deeper and deeper. Sherman was certain they were headed for a drop the likes of Niagara Falls, when the boat suddenly wrenched itself out of the powerful current and slowed down. They emerged from the fog and docked at what looked like the wooden posts of a deserted port.

The ferryman turned his skeletal face toward Sherman. His bony jaw unhinged and he croaked in a voice more dead than alive, "Pay the ferryman."

"What's the fare?" asked Sherman, fearing the worst.

Phlegyas opened the folds of his tattered cloak and revealed the gilded handle of a dagger that was lodged in his ribs.

"A piece of gold or a pint of blood." He drew the dagger from his chest and pointed it at Sherman's neck. "Whatever you can more easily afford," he moaned.

"Gold?" shrieked Billie clambering for Virgil and grabbing him by the scruff of the neck. "You knew we needed *gold*, you little sneak of an elf!"

"It's all right Billie," Sherman said quickly. "We have the necklace."

"No," said Virgil, squirming out of Billie's grasp. He ducked into the far corner of the barge.

"I claim the necklace in fulfillment of your promise. One promise to do as I ask when I ask it. I take the necklace and I take it now."

"Not a chance!" shouted Billie. "You knew from the start we needed that stone, you manipulative little twerp. You'll get it over my dead body."

"Dead or alive—makes no difference to the promise," said Virgil.

Billie lunged for him, but he stopped her, saying, "And either way, I did not ask you for the stone. You keep the stone, but the gold chain is mine."

"We're not giving you the necklace, and that's final," said Billie.

"Give it to him," sighed Sherman. "A deal is a deal."

"Then what are we supposed to do?" asked Billie. "Pay with blood?"

"It's okay," said Sherman. "We've got another piece of gold."

chapter twenty-one

Without taking her eyes off of Virgil, Billie undid the necklace. She unhooked the pendant from the gold chain and shoved the stone deep into the pocket of her jeans. She tossed the links to Virgil. He caught the chain and squealed.

Sherman clicked open his violin case. He withdrew Stella's diary. It now contained nothing more than page after page of circles.

He jammed his finger into the spine. He pushed out the thin gold pen that he had lodged there earlier. The inscription was not visible.

Sherman extended a trembling hand toward Phlegyas. When the ferryman spied the glimmer of gold, he slipped the dagger back into his breastbone and seized the thin gold rod with his gaunt fingers. Then, in one fleet motion, he cast it high into the fog over the rushing river.

"Quickly!" shouted Virgil, clambering for the dock. "Exit before the gold touches the blood."

Billie leaped onto the wobbly planks. She swung round to help Sherman. He snatched his violin case and lunged for the dock. Sherman nearly fell into the river, but Billie caught him and yanked him over the edge just as the gold pen hit the river's surface.

As it plunged into the bubbling brine, the barge pushed off from the dock. It immediately disappeared into the heavy fog. The low moan of the foghorn echoed in the distance.

"Close call," sighed Billie, clinging to Drake's clock.

She had lost her glow stick. She hastily retrieved another from her pocket and snapped it. The violet light hugged the thick fog. It made Billie feel like she was swimming in a sea of cotton candy. She swatted the pink mist from her face.

"I think I dropped one of your slippers, Germ."

"Oh good. I'm glad you didn't drop anything *useful*...like *your head*," said Sherman, grudgingly accepting he'd be barefoot for the remainder of the journey. His left foot had grazed the waters. When he looked down he saw that his toes were stained a deep scarlet. He wiped his foot against the dry surface of the dock, but the mark didn't even smudge.

Vigil did a flip in the air, landing with a thud on the rickety dock.

"I have it! I have it!" he sang as he swung the gold necklace in the air.

"What are you so cheery about, stupid sprite?" asked Billie. "You stole our necklace and nearly cost us our lives."

A pointy-tooth grin distorted Virgil's face. Shivers paraded up Sherman's spine.

"I have it! I have it—at last!" Virgil hooted. "Link by link, I shall bring the others home!"

"*Others?*" asked Sherman. "What *others*, Virgil?"

The white dwarf drew in close.

"The slaves of *Al*," he said in a mysterious hushed voice.

"Who in the world is Al?" asked Billie. "Some friend of yours?"

"Ha! Ha!" Virgil twittered. "You shall soon find out! This is the Fourth Circle—the City of Nix. I have fulfilled my end of the bargain. I have brought you here. Now, you are on your own."

"Not so fast, buddy," said Billie. "You said you'd bring us *through* the Fourth Circle, not *to* it. You still owe us."

"I said *to—to* the Fourth Circle," insisted Virgil. "I am no longer obliged to continue."

"I'm afraid Billie's right," said Sherman. "We said *through* the Fourth Circle and you agreed. We've kept our word. You are still bound to us by yours."

Virgil paused for a moment to think. As the recollection hit him, he began stamping his feet on the dock like a spoiled toddler. "You tricked me! You cheated me!"

"Looks like *someone's* a sore loser," grinned Billie. "The deal was done fair and square. Now guide us, you gremlin, or I'll repossess the necklace because you shirked on your end of the bargain."

Virgil snarled and then stomped off the dock and out of the fog with Sherman and Billie at his heels. As they left the rocky banks of the River of Woe, the air grew less pungent and the haze evaporated.

Sherman found himself walking along a cobblestone road laid through what looked like desert on either side. Huge boulders, dry brush and small cacti dotted the arid landscape. Strange trees with raised limbs sprouted spiky leaves. The irregular outlines were spooky. They resembled gnarled, deformed fingers with dagger-like tufts emerging from the tips.

The cobblestones felt cool against the soles of Sherman's feet. He was thankful the road was more forgiving than what lay at the end of it.

In the distance, an enormous wall rose, stark and foreboding. As the group advanced, Sherman could see that the wall was much higher than those he and Billie had scaled in the Second Circle. Within the enclosure rose the silhouette of a great turreted castle. The last castle Sherman had entered had been Umbra's castle, Imwratheer, which had bulldozer-sized beetles as watchdogs.

As he approached the wall, Sherman saw the road ended at an archway. Enormous wooden doors barred any access.

"The entrance to the City of Nix," said Virgil pointing at the doors. "The steps that descend to the Fifth Circle lie at the far end of the Palace of Al, behind the great wizard's throne. I will take you there in fulfillment of my promise, but ask me no questions—no matter what you may see."

Sherman took a deep breath.

"How do we get inside?" he whispered.

Virgil cast him a devious sideways glance that said, *Watch this*. Then he stood stock-still, facing the giant doors. He began to hum. It was a ghostly high-pitched note, like the sound of someone blowing through tissue paper wrapped over a comb. It reverberated from the whole of his being and rippled outward like sonar waves.

Billie watched with narrow eyes and a suspicious scowl.

"What's the dwarf doing?" she mouthed to Sherman.

He raised his eyebrows and shrugged his shoulders in response.

Soon Virgil's single note was joined by more of various pitches, creating an eerie cacophonous din. As the noise grew louder, Sherman heard a clicking sound. Rusty hinges screeched as the huge doors swung wide.

"How'd you do—," Sherman was about to ask, then cupped a hand to his mouth as Virgil shot him an angry look.

"No questions. Got it."

Something about the opening in the wall reminded Sherman of an enormous mouth poised to swallow him. His insides trembled, but he steadied his nerves. *It's the only way*, he told himself. *There's no turning back.*

As he slipped through the yawning archway, he noticed something white flash into the shadows. He dropped his glow stick and it rolled into a crack.

Was that what I think it was? he wondered, but

he stopped himself before the question slipped past his lips.

Virgil unhooked link after link of Stella's gold chain until it clinked in his hands like a pile of loose change. He quickly tossed one of the links into the shadows and Sherman heard something scramble after it.

"You're doing it again, troll," said Billie brandishing a fist in Virgil's face. "You're hiding stuff from us."

"*Dwarf!*" Virgil threatened with a fierce scowl. "And you agreed not to ask any questions!"

"*He* agreed," said Billie tilting her head toward Sherman. "*I* didn't. But don't worry Virge, that was a statement, not a question."

Another flash of white scuttled off behind them and then the great doors creaked shut. Sherman took a deep breath and reached into his pocket. He withdrew another glow stick—his last. He snapped it and a bright neon-green light illuminated the dark tunnel. He took several steps, until he was through the thick wall. On the other side, he saw a crude town of rickety wooden dwellings. They rose unevenly, leaning and tilting in all directions.

"The City of Nix," he sighed.

"More like City of Sticks," said Billie over his shoulder.

Sherman looked at Billie, and then at the road ahead. It appeared to curve through the deserted village toward the doors of the palace.

Out of the corner of his eye, Sherman caught a glimpse of yet another flash of white. He thought he saw it dart into the shadows between two of the structures.

Virgil tossed a gold link to something hiding there as though he were tossing crumbs to a pigeon. Sherman shook his head and shuffled forward, holding back questions that were desperately trying to force their way out. As they made their way through the derelict village, Virgil scurried ahead, tossing links here, there and everywhere.

A narrow moat set the castle off from the rest of the town. An enormous wooden drawbridge was lowered across the stale, swampy waters. The group crossed the bridge in silence.

They stood at the doorway of the great stone palace. The smooth façade looked like marble—cold and hard—not the least bit inviting.

As they passed through the doorway and into a giant vestibule, a hush filled the air, as though the walls were padded foam instead of solid stone. There not a stick of furniture in sight, just enormous pillars stretching up to the ceiling and huge paintings adorning every wall. From a distance, they all appeared the same. Sherman approached one of the canvases to have a better look.

The painting's solid black background took on a greenish tinge from Sherman's glow stick. In the center was a star-shaped mass of exploding light. It looked like it had plunged through another mass, sending light splattering outward. Beneath the giant portrait was a caption that read: IRAS04505-2958.

What in the world? thought Sherman, but Billie was quick with answers.

"It's a quasar," she said. "A huge energy source. Roger's shown me pictures of 'em taken by the Hubble Space telescope. No one's really sure how they're formed, but there's usually a supermassive black hole nearby."

"You can stop with the brothers already," said Sherman. "I know your little secret. It's all you, Billie…isn't it?"

Before Billie could respond, another flash of white darted from one column to another. Virgil flung a link that *clink-clinked* across the marble floor. A hand remarkably similar to Virgil's reached out from behind the stone pillar, snatched up the gold and disappeared again.

Sherman's eyes shot at Virgil. Virgil grinned

like a cat in a canary cage.

"Lead on," said Sherman, pointing his glow stick toward the far end of the vestibule. He saw six archways and just as many staircases rising above them.

"The castle is a winding labyrinth of corridors, tunnels and stairwells. Remain close, or you shall have to navigate your way on your own," said Virgil.

He began humming again. Each time a new sound responded, Virgil moved in that direction. Then, he lobbed a gold link into the shadows. It was quickly snatched up by mysterious white hands.

Steadily, the group snaked their way through the many corridors, stairwells, archways and doors. The palace seemed never-ending. Sherman thought they would wander forever. The floor was smooth and cold, and he stumbled more than once where one slab of marble butted up against another.

Virgil and Billie moved swiftly ahead toward a row of seven doors. Sherman's violin case slipped through his grasp and he bent to pick it up. By the time he righted himself, Virgil and Billie had vanished.

"Hey!" he shouted, trying to catch up. "Wait!" But it was too late. They were gone.

Sherman ran up and down the corridor searching behind each door. Panic squeezed his lungs. He tried to call out, but his voice was caught behind the lump of bile in his throat.

What now? Where do I go? The Spirit Stone... can Billie make it alone?

Sherman closed his eyes and willed his heartbeat to slow. He summoned any remnants of courage still in him.

Think. Think. There's got to be a way to find them. If only I could imitate Virgil's sound. Maybe he'll hear me, and answer...

Sherman tried hard to hum, but all he could produce was a dry squeak. He tried again. This time he sounded more like a cow mooing.

Frustrated, he gave up and opened his eyes.

He was staring at his violin case.

Of course. Why didn't I think of this before?

He snapped open the case and, resting the glow stick on the ground, he withdrew his trusty instrument. He took a deep breath and placed the Stradivarius under his chin. Holding the bow in position, he closed his eyes. The bow glided across the strings, singing one long perfect note. Vibrato.

Sherman had perfect pitch and he hit the D minor that Virgil hummed dead-on. It echoed through the corridor. Sherman stopped and waited. He held his breath, straining his ears for a response, but none came. He swallowed his disappointment.

What would Ms Wong say? What she always says: Don't play the violin, Sherman. Let it play you.

He emptied his mind and steadied his nerves. He tried again.

This time, the sound that poured from the instrument was like a melodious plea. Sherman was expecting Virgil's single note to return his call, but what erupted from behind one of the doors was more like a symphony.

It was mesmerizing, and the sound drew Sherman toward it with invisible strings. The song came from the doorway farthest to the left.

Sherman had lucked out once before with a door on the left. He gently patted his violin as if to say, *finally, you've done something useful.* Then he packed it away. He picked up his glow stick and slipped through the door.

The corridor descended sharply. The symphony had ended, but Sherman now heard a faint noise in the distance, like the churning and grinding of some kind of machinery.

As the corridor began to fall more rapidly, Sherman took tiny steps to keep himself upright. He contemplated turning back, but the floor dipped so suddenly he slid straight down. He shut his eyes, clung to his violin case and clenched his last glow stick tightly as he slid down the shaft toward the mysterious sound.

The chute spat him out onto a rocky surface. The noise was almost deafening. He resisted the urge to cover his ears. He sat for a moment catching his breath, and then finger by finger, he released the light that was trapped in his clenched fist.

Sherman was in a cavern the size of a hockey arena. An intricate puzzle of wooden levers, wheels, axles, pulleys and gears churned from within. The colossal machine was operated by hundreds of white dwarves that all resembled Virgil, from their thick wiry hair, to the tips of their pointed shoes.

At first, no one noticed Sherman. Then one by one all eyes were drawn to him.

"So this was what Virgil meant by *the others*," he whispered to himself.

The nearest dwarf perked up at the mention of Virgil's name. He let go of the lever he was exerting force on and timidly approached Sherman.

"You mentioned Virgil. Do you know him?"

Sherman cleared his throat. He shouted to be heard over the hum of the machine.

"I do. It was Virgil who led me here."

Several other dwarves drew near. Sherman

was surrounded by an army of little people all looking toward him as though he were some sort of wonder.

"If Virgil has come, then we must be saved," one said. "He promised only to return when he could free us from slavery."

Saved?

It all started to make sense to Sherman. In Limbo Forest, Virgil had said he was the last of the great white dwarves. He had claimed the gold necklace and had been handing out links.

"You need gold to use Phlegyas' ferry," Sherman muttered to himself. "Without gold, you're stuck." He took a deep breath. "Are you slaves of Al?"

Several dwarves nodded sadly. One spoke out.

"We were lured here with promise of riches. We left the peace of our beautiful forest behind and have been made to run the machine that stabilizes the wormhole."

"*The wormhole?*" asked Sherman.

"Yes. A tunnel in space."

"It is an endless task," sighed another.

Sherman thought about this for a moment. In grade five, his class visited the local science center. It had an exhibit on wormholes. Sherman remembered they were spinning black holes that served as bridges from one time to another. You could use them to travel through time and space.

The downside of wormholes was that even if you could find one, they were very unstable. The doorways at either end would snap shut if any disturbance entered. The only way to reverse the effect and keep the wormhole open would be to create a counter-disturbance that would cancel out the first one.

Sherman furrowed his brow. There was more.

What had that guide at the science center said? Sherman struggled to remember.

Oh yeah! She said you'd need an entire civilization just to monitor the tunnel and keep it open.

Obviously this Al, whoever he was, had found his *entire civilization.* He was forcing the white dwarves to create the counter-disturbance needed to cancel out all other disturbances and keep the tunnel open.

"Help me find Al," said Sherman, "and I will help you find Virgil. He has brought you some gold to pay your fare back home."

A cheer erupted and many dwarves danced and did flips.

"We are saved! We are saved!" they chanted.

Three dwarves pulled Sherman to his feet and led him toward the far end of the cavern. There, a ladder, at least a hundred feet tall, disappeared through a small hole in the ceiling.

Sherman gulped. He was not good with heights and the ladder looked wobbly.

This is nothing for the Shermanosaurus! He scales ladders twice this height blindfolded and with one hand tied behind his back!

Sherman transferred the glow stick to the hand that held his violin case. With only one free hand, he began to pull himself up, rung by rung. About halfway, the glow stick slipped from his grasp. Since several white dwarves were already behind him on the ladder, there was no turning back. From its glow he could still make out the small hole at the top. He forced himself to continue with slow, steady steps.

His head peeked through the opening. He was in complete darkness.

Sherman took a deep breath and pulled himself and his violin case through the hole. He checked his pockets, but they were empty. He'd lost the final glow stick.

Inch by inch he crawled across the stone floor. Then suddenly, a voice echoed through the chamber.

"Well, well, well, what do we have here?"

chapter twenty-two

Drake grasped the enormous sword in his trembling hands. The blade felt like it weighed a hundred pounds. Pearls of sweat formed on his forehead and slid down his face. His breathing was heavy and loud.

It's now or never, he thought. *I must do it and do it quickly.*

"My sentiments exactly," said Umbra, misinterpreting Drake's thoughts. "Do what you were meant to do, Drake Livingstone. Or should I say, *Evil Darking Stone.* Destroy the light, for once and all eternity!"

Drake hoisted the sword high above his head.

"It would be a rash act," said a small voice from inside the spider's capsule. The voice was low and breathless, but familiar.

Drake's heart somersaulted. *It was his sister! It was Stella! She was real and she was here! At least...it* sounded *like her.*

"Silence!" commanded Umbra. "Hold your tongue, or your death will be slow and excruciating, rather than swift."

"Nonsense!" said the voice. "You have no power over me. You never have and you never will."

Drake was now certain the voice belonged to Stella. She sounded weak and out of breath.

Tears welled in Drake's eyes. He steadied the weight that quivered above him. His muscles ached with the burden.

Not yet. Stick to the plan.

"That is right, Drake. Remain faithful to our design," said Umbra. "Plunge the sword through her heart and fulfill your destiny."

"You have once again miscalculated," said the voice in the capsule. "Surrender now, Umbra, or suffer my wrath."

Cold rage calmed the evil creature.

"Surrender? Me?" Umbra scoffed. "A ridiculous notion under the circumstances, do you not think." He drew the hood of his cloak back over his pulsing skull. His breathing was slow and calculated.

"You merely barter for time," he sneered. "But there is none to be had. It is all over. Drake will complete his task. You know he will. He will plunge the sword downward. I have foreseen it."

"Perhaps," said Stella's voice.

Drake marveled. She seemed to have unusual confidence given the circumstances.

"Perhaps it has been my design that Drake obey your command," she continued. "Perhaps it is *my will* not *yours*, that he let the sword fall."

"You speak in riddles. You wish only to trick me," sighed Umbra, clicking his long nails. "You have duped me before, but not this time." He turned his steely eyes toward Drake.

"She is weak. She is dying. But we will not let her go peacefully. Do it now. Thrust the sword into the spider's capsule. It is what you were born to do."

Drake stood motionless. The weight of the universe bore down on him. His mind was a tangled mess. His body swayed under the burden. He could not hold it much longer. His throat went dry and his body so cold he no longer felt his limbs.

Can't...not here...not now...

The Obelisk!

It came to him like a dream out of the fog. Before he knew it the words were out.

"Let us take her to the Obelisk, great and glorious Shadowmaster," he said. "It is dark now. No longer a threat to either of us. Let us do the deed there. It will be symbolic of your conquest and of her ultimate defeat!"

Drake shivered as Umbra's mind collided with his own. He felt Umbra inside his head searching his motives. It was like they were no longer two beings but one. Even Drake's words were no longer his own. He spoke like Umbra now. He looked like Umbra. He was losing himself. He was becoming the shadow.

Drake held his breath and froze his mind. For a second, Umbra remained still and Drake was certain his thoughts had betrayed his true intentions.

"The Obelisk is a beacon of hope," said Stella's voice. "You can no more destroy *hope* than you can destroy *light*. You have no power there, Umbra. Heed my warning."

Umbra's maniacal laughter echoed through the towers of Imwratheer. Drake cringed at the sight of his crooked black teeth.

He turned to Drake. "Yessss. The beacon of hope will become a symbol of defeat. No light shall shine there evermore. The Bright Side is finished. They are all Blacklands from now until forever!"

Drake's heart leapt. *A little time. Just a little.* "Very little time." Umbra reached down and lifted the sword from Drake's trembling hands and returned it to the folds of his tattered garb.

With a flick of his bony hand he summoned the

Shadowbands. Umbra instructed them to drag Spinneret's silken capsule.

"Take her to the Obelisk," he commanded. "It will all end there."

chapter twenty-three

Sherman took a deep breath. He was about to say something when a violet light illuminated the long narrow chamber and a familiar voice whispered in his ear.

"Hiya, Worm! Where'd you disappear to?"

Sherman swung round. He was so glad to see Billie, he dropped his violin case and hugged her with both arms. She shoved him away.

"Watch it, Germ! You're in my personal space!"

Over Billie's shoulder, Sherman saw several white dwarves congregate around Virgil. He flashed a handful of gold.

A crash of thunder interrupted the reunion.

"At long last! Come, come! I have been expecting you!" said a shaky voice.

Sherman swung round. His jaw dropped. He was expecting to see a wizard of some sort sitting upon a gilded throne. What he saw was nothing remotely similar.

At the far end of the otherwise empty chamber there was a huge wooden desk. A small man was seated in a leather swivel chair behind it. The desk was strewn with clumps of papers, pieces of chalk, text books and notebooks. Behind the desk was an enormous blackboard with mathematical equations and formulae scribbled in all directions. The blackboard was framed by two enormous bookshelves cluttered with more papers, binders and books. The disarray reminded Sherman of his own room.

The old man had unruly white hair as though it were permanently wind-blown. Bushy black eyebrows accentuated the laugh wrinkles that creased the corners of his eyes. His mouth twitched beneath a thick, silver moustache.

Sherman couldn't help but gawk.

He's the spitting image of... No. It can't be.

"At long last, travelers arrive at my wormhole!" said the old man. He rose to his feet and extended both hands.

"Wormhole!" chuckled Billie, elbowing Sherman. "Get it, *Worm? You're* in a *wormhole?*"

"Stop babbling," snapped the old man. "Identify,

classify, and label yourselves."

Okaaay, thought Sherman. *This guy is definitely no wizard. More like some wacky scientist with a few brain cells missing nuclei. Still, he looks so much like...*

"Billie's the name." She gave a mock salute.

"I'm Sherman," he mumbled.

The old man eyed Billie's glow stick.

"I see you have brought your host a gift. Come, come. Bring me that stick of light," said the old man. "I have never seen anything quite like it. And I daresay we are much in need of light in this dark tunnel."

Billie didn't move. She contemplated the glow stick in her hand.

"Give it to him," Sherman whispered through clenched teeth. "I don't think this guy is all there, if you know what I mean."

Billie paused, sizing the old man up and down before swaggering toward his desk. She extended her hand across the piles of paper, but just as the old man reached for the glow stick she snatched it back.

"Not so fast, buddy," she grinned.

A crash of thunder forced Sherman's eyes shut. He opened one.

"Come, come," said Al. "Give me that light or

I shall split you like an atom!"

"You can split your pants if you want," said Billie. "I'll give you the light when I'm good and ready."

There's bravery… thought Sherman, opening his other eye, *and then there's stupidity…I just can't figure her out!*

The next crash of thunder shook the entire palace and Sherman was sure they were done for.

"Don't get your photons and neutrons all in a twist," said Billie. "This light's all yours. Just point us to the stairs that'll take us to the next level. We've got a Spirit Stone to return."

"It's the answer to setting everything right," added Sherman quickly. "Bringing back the light and righting the past."

"Ha!" The old man burst out laughing. "The past? No such thing! Time is relative. It is all happening at once. All you need is to pass from one time to another…one universe to another…and wormholes are the answer. Isn't that why you are here?" The old man's voice trailed off.

Out of the corner of his eye, Sherman saw Virgil handing out gold links, nodding and gesturing to the other dwarves. They crept toward the hole in the floor, a single gold link glistening in the palm of each white hand.

Apparently, Al saw them too.

Another crash of thunder stopped them in their tracks.

"Gold?" said Al, his pitch rising wildly. "You fools! You brought *gold* to the white dwarves?" He clutched his hair out of frustration. "Do you know what this means?"

Sherman looked at Billie and then at Virgil. Virgil puffed out his chest and raised his chin.

"It is over, Al," said Virgil. "You cannot hold us here against our will any longer."

The old man squeezed his eyes shut. Then he let out a sigh that was more sad than angry.

"You naïve fools." He shook his fist at Sherman and Billie. "You have no idea what you've done. The dwarves power the machine that I have designed to create the counter disturbance in the spacetime structure. The counter disturbance is needed to keep this wormhole open. If it is not upheld, the wormhole will shut and you will be trapped here forever. When the dwarves leave, it is all over. I cannot hold them here now that they possess the fare home."

Trembling, he sunk into his chair and dropped his head to his desk.

"So long…so close…and this is how it ends…"

Sherman turned to Virgil. "Is it true?"

The white dwarf bobbed his chin.

"The time has come. My people will return home to Limbo Forest where they belong."

Billie took a step toward Virgil with teeth and fists clenched.

"That's it! Let me at him! He lied to us from the start! He knew exactly what he was doing, the little conniving pixie."

For the billionth time Sherman was forced to restrain her.

"Let him go, Billie. There's nothing you or I can do to stop them now." Realizing Sherman was right, she stopped struggling. He let her go.

"Virgil," continued Sherman, "you have your freedom, but you won't all fit in the ferry at the same time. Can't your people power the machine a little while longer? All we need is a little more time."

Virgil contemplated Sherman's words. "You have been just with me from the start. We will board the boat ten at a time. The machine will keep turning until the last group leaves. That is all I can promise."

Sherman hoped Virgil would keep his word, but it still meant they had to hurry.

He turned toward the small man slumped over his desk.

"Please. We need to get to the Gorge and

replace this Spirit Stone, before it's too late. Will you help us?"

The old man lifted his head and smoothed back his silver hair. Defeat welled in his eyes.

"My work was all theory until I found my way here. I needed a civilization that could keep the tunnel from collapsing. I envisioned great travelers passing through. From the future to the past. From one universe to another."

He shook his head and continued bitterly. "And now it seems, you two are the first and last to use this bridge. Once the machine stops, the doors will snap shut. Perhaps forever."

"Can you tell us what comes after here?" asked Billie.

"One more circle and then the Gorge. You'll find the exit to the wormhole in the center of the Spirit Stones. Where that exit leads I cannot say, for I have remained here overseeing the stabilization of the Wormhole for what seems like an eternity."

"Where are the stairs?" asked Billie.

The old man ambled to the bookshelf on his right. He ran his hand along the bottom of the third shelf and it creaked open, revealing a dark stairwell. He motioned for Sherman and Billie to enter. They approached the doorway, but Sherman stopped short and turned to Virgil one last time.

"Will you keep your word?" he asked.

The white dwarf nodded his head.

Billie was already inside the stairwell surveying it with her chemical torch. Sherman ducked inside and then turned back toward Al.

"Come with us!" he said. "There's nothing for you here now."

The old man shook his head.

"Even if the tunnel snaps shut, perhaps I can figure out a way to open it again." He turned to face his blackboard, staring at the equations that zigzagged across it. And then he frantically erased them all and began feverishly writing anew, muttering and babbling to himself, thunder rolling like a distant storm.

Billie reached into her pocket and withdrew her remaining two glow sticks.

"Hey, catch!" she shouted through the doorway as she tossed them to Al. "Deal's a deal. I always keep my promises," she said, winking at Sherman.

Al stopped scribbling long enough to catch the glow sticks. He examined them for a moment, smiled, and then he tucked them into his pocket. He returned to his math.

Sherman and Billie took several steps down the narrow tunnel. The bookcase slammed shut behind them.

chapter twenty-four

Drake soared through the darkness, as though tied to Umbra by invisible strings. They glided like phantoms through the Sandmaze, across Murk Sea, over Gloom Forest and Bone Desert. In what felt like no time at all, they reached the gaping fissure that split the Halfstone and marked the boundary between the Bright Side and the Blacklands. There, they stopped.

Umbra had never set foot on the other side of his world. Drake sensed his apprehension and Umbra shot him a look brimming with unbridled fury. To prove himself, Umbra plunged his foot down on the Bright Side. He left a cavernous impression in the rock.

As they crossed the border, a burning sensation made the blood in Drake's veins sizzle. The pain he felt came from Umbra. Although all light was gone, Aura was not yet dead and the Bright Side maintained a glimmer of its former magic.

"It is our world now, Drake," Umbra said, triumphantly. He swallowed the sting and plowed further and further into the heart of the Bright Side, halting only when he reached the base of the Crystal Obelisk. The glass structure, now dark, erupted from the ground and rocketed skyward.

"It is all ours, Drake. The entire universe is at our command. You have chosen wisely. Better to triumph with me, than perish alongside your sister."

Drake nodded feebly. He stared up at the hollow shell of the former tower of light. It was like a cocoon long abandoned. Even to his keen sense of sight, it was now almost invisible.

"There is an opening in the east," said the weak voice that was both Stella and Aura.

"See now," chuckled Umbra. "She even helps us destroy her!"

That's crazy! Why would she help him destroy her? thought Drake. *Is Umbra already so drunk with power that he's not even questioning this?*

Umbra motioned to the Shadowbands to drag the capsule toward the entrance. He gave Drake's thoughts a half-hearted response.

"She realizes at long last her reign is over."

Something was up, but Drake nodded, swallowing his thoughts and emotions. He'd soon have to make a decision. His eyelids blinked back tears.

Drake trailed behind the army of black phantoms as they streamed into a small circular opening at the base of the glass structure. The Shadowbands wheezed and hissed in delight. Passing through the threshold of the Obelisk was a declaration of victory.

They were in the heart of the glass tower. It was an odd place—just an empty glass tube. Drake suddenly felt like a bug held prisoner under a drinking glass.

How far up does the tower stretch? Where does it end? he wondered.

"It no longer matters," said Umbra answering Drake's thoughts. "Wherever the tip of the Obelisk leads, it is all ours now. A vast sea of darkness for us to explore and enjoy for all eternity."

Umbra drew the great sword from the folds of his cloak. With a look of maniacal pleasure distorting his already hideous face, he held it out toward Drake.

Drake took a deep breath and grasped the handle. His heart pounded and his head ached as his thoughts drifted from him...

It was a crisp day in January. Drake, Stella

and Sherman were wearing cheap sunglasses with developed film pasted over top. They were standing in a hidden grove of cedar trees in the woods behind their school. They were looking up into the sky, watching with bated breath as the dark surface of the moon slowly slid across the sun, swallowing all light. The shadow of the moon slithered across the ground at their feet. It was the solar eclipse. It was the beginning...

"Yes, the beginning," sighed Umbra. "The beginning of *the end...*"

Drake's heart hammered against his ribcage. He was out of time. Panic whirled like a tornado inside his head spinning him out of control. His stomach lurched. His body quivered and he swayed from side to side.

How he wished the eclipse had never happened. That he had never traveled through the light. That he had never met Umbra or Aura. How he wished he could change the past—undo it all. Everything. Every last second of it.

And there it was. A simple thought slipping free from the tangle in his mind.

Make a change and make it now!

Drake's thought had only begun to take shape when Stella's voice shattered it.

"Do it!" she whispered. "Quickly! Before the circle closes forever."

Do it? Do what? You can't mean...you can't want me to...

Drake's head felt like it was going to explode. He couldn't think anymore. He couldn't breath. A million images zipped through his mind at supersonic speed.

He squeezed his eyes shut and willed himself still. And suddenly, as though a great storm had passed, he stopped shaking. His heartbeat slowed. His mind focused. And when he opened his eyes again, he knew exactly what must be done.

Umbra is right. Stella is right. I must strike now. It's the only way.

Drake hoisted the sword as high as he could. His muscles would have ached under the burden were he not so numb. Out of the corner of his eye, he saw Umbra's demented grin urging him on.

It's the only way.

He took a deep breath and shut his eyes. He couldn't watch. Tears spilled down his cheeks.

With unearthly strength, he plunged the blade downward. It pierced the tightly bound silk capsule as though it were tissue. The floor beneath him trembled as the sword rammed right through the base of the Obelisk.

It was done.

Seconds passed like hours. Drake opened his eyes. The capsule had split in two perfect halves. And there, lying inside, was the lifeless body of his sister, Stella. She still wore the same snow pants and ski jacket he'd last seen her in all those months ago. She looked eerily similar, the only difference being the cavernous hole where her heart should have been.

Drake's breath caught in his throat as his mind scrambled to catch up to what his eyes beheld and in the second he understood, his hands flew to his head, ripping and tearing at his hair.

No! Not this! This is wrong! All wrong!

Life drained from him like water through a sieve. His knees folded and he collapsed on top of Stella's limp body.

"No!" he wailed. "No!"

Bile rose in his throat. He gagged and coughed and sputtered.

Shrieks of triumph filled the air as Shadowbands slithered and coiled around the broken capsule.

"What have I done, Stella?" sobbed Drake. He buried his face in the folds of her jacket. "What have I done?"

Umbra's voice sliced though the chaos. "You

have done what you were born to do."

Drake lifted his head. Hate swelled within him. It rose like a flood and dragged him off in its violent current.

chapter twenty-five

Sherman and Billie struggled to make their way down uneven steps that reminded them of the vertebrae of some prehistoric monster. A powerful gust of wind kept sucking them back up a few steps. Then it would rush past them from behind and send them practically head over heels deeper down the staircase. They had to be even more cautious because the walls were slimy and they would not provide a solid grip should they stumble. With only the violet light as their guide, they pressed themselves hard until they reached the bottom. Sherman gasped for air. He stopped for a moment to catch his breath.

"Need...to....keep...moving," he sputtered between gulps of air. He pushed Billie onward with his free hand.

The dank stairwell opened up into an enormous curving cave. Like the walls of the stairwell, the ground felt wet and spongy. It appeared pink in the glow of Billie's light.

Sherman cringed and wrinkled his bare toes. He regretted more than ever the loss of his footwear.

Running across this ground is like racing across a slice of salami.

He moved as quickly as he could, each step making a squishy, sucking sound.

Suddenly the floor wobbled like jelly. "Whoa!" he gasped, holding out his arms for balance. His violin case nearly tipped him over. "Earthquake!"

"We're not on the earth anymore, Worm. Remember?" said Billie steadying herself.

The floor of the cave settled.

"Good point," said Sherman.

He eyed the cavern with heightened suspicion. Something was definitely off here, but he couldn't quite place what it was. *No time to wonder. Got to keep moving.*

The air was appallingly humid and a hot wind kept rushing past Sherman. An overpowering smell hung thick in the air, like something dead lay rotting nearby. The place gave Sherman the creeps.

Something's really wrong here...

"Pick up the pace," he said, jogging up to meet Billie. "I have a bad feeling about this cave."

As the tunnel curved, Sherman noticed stalagmites and stalactites sprouted in two neat rows, from the ceiling and floor, but only along the sides of the cave. In the distance he could see an opening. The spiky rocks continued all the way around, forming a complete semi-circle blocking his way like the bars of a cage.

In the distance, he saw an opening.

"This can't already be the end of this circle?" asked Sherman.

"Looks like it," said Billie. "Everything's shrinking."

Sherman recalled now that each Circle they descended into had been smaller than the previous. This cave was only the size of a subway tunnel.

"Will we be able to squeeze between those spiky rocks?" Sherman asked, pointing to the row of sharp stalagmites and stalactites obstructing their exit.

"No probs," said Billie. "Should be enough space." She poked Sherman in the gut. "Course for you, Worm, we'll need to find one that's extra wide."

"Ha, ha. Very funny," said Sherman. "You need one that's extra wide too—to fit your big blockhead through!"

Billie's grin morphed into a hurt look. She turned and strode ahead. Sherman suddenly wished he could take back what he'd just said.

"Aw, come on, Billie," he yelled, lumbering up

to her and punching her in the arm. "I didn't mean it. Really." She cast him a sideways glance that contained more venom than two hundred rattle snakes. "In fact," he added quickly, "I think, er,…I mean, er,…what I'm trying to say is…I think you're kind of…actually…pretty."

The last words dangled in the air, blowing in the breeze. It felt like an eternity before Billie responded. She looked at Sherman again, only this time he was relieved to see the venom was gone. Her look was softer and it seemed to say, *Thanks, Worm.*

Sherman's cheeks flushed ruby-red. It was a good thing there wasn't much light and no time for awkward moments. He willed his focus back to the Spirit Stone.

"The wormhole's going to snap shut soon. We've got to move quicker." As he spoke, the ground wriggled again and he lost his balance. He fell flat on his face into the squishy slimy ground.

"Eeww!" he spat. "This feels like…like a… like a…"

But before he could finish his sentence, the whole cave began to shift. The ceiling lifted and the floor dropped. The stalactites and stalagmites separated and a huge rush of air sucked Billie backward. She fell on her back.

"It's a…it's a…" Sherman sputtered.

"A MOOOUUUTH!" yelled Billie. She rolled over and crawled as fast as she could toward Sherman, clock and glow stick in hand, but suddenly the inward rush of air changed direction. With the force of a hurricane, the huge mouth sneezed and Billie and Sherman were propelled out into an abyss of darkness at what felt like the speed of light.

Sherman shut his eyes. He clung to his violin case with one hand and Billie's foot with the other.

"What….was…that?" he hollered as he plummeted through emptiness.

For a split second, he wondered if he might just fall forever but the thought was knocked out of him when he hit hard, lumpy ground. He lay there for a moment catching his breath. *City of Nix? What kind of creature is a Nix?* Then a horrible image streaked through his brain. *Imagine being swallowed by some gruesome creature and then being digested throughout eternity.* He shivered and shook his head. Something kicked his leg.

One by one, he opened his eyes. Billie was standing beside him holding her glow stick up like a torch.

Sherman's jaw dropped. In the violet light he saw an enormous circular canyon. Underneath him, beside him and as far as the weak light carried, lay billions of smooth, round rocks, like a sea of black pearls the size of grapefruit. There was stillness in the air. Serenity oozed over him like syrup. All panic and fear evaporated. He could hear a distant trickle of water and he saw a glistening pool in the center of the stones. He wondered if this was where the River of Woe emptied. There was no offensive odor here, but rather a freshness, a newness, like the smell of dew on an early spring morning.

"The *uh uh* Gorge *orge orge*," said Sherman. His voice echoed outward like a ripple in a pond. "These *ese ese* are *are are* all *all all* Spirit *irit irit* Stones *ones ones*..."

"What *at at?*" asked Billie. "Echo's *echo's echo's* too *oo oo* confusing *using using*..."

Each word they spoke seemed to travel round the gorge in a circle leaving their lips and then scooting past their ears over and over again.

"Don't *on't on't* talk *alk alk*..." said Sherman. He reached underneath him and picked up a Spirit Stone. It was heavy and light at the same time. It felt odd in his hands—like it was some-how...*alive.* Etched onto it was something in a language he couldn't understand. He picked up another then another and another. They all had inscriptions and each was unique. Some looked like letters in languages he didn't understand, while others looked like symbols or numbers or just lines.

He motioned for Billie to extract the small stone from her pocket. She tucked Drake's clock into her coat pocket and dug into her jeans. She withdrew Stella's pendant and held it up to the glow stick. It was a perfect miniature replica of the enormous Spirit Stones that filled the canyon.

Sherman set the stone he was holding back onto the heap and pointed to the masses. Then he raised his palms upward as if to say, *How will we ever find the right one?*

As if in answer to his question, he saw the tiniest flicker of light in the distance over Billie's shoulder. He blinked hard, and then the flicker was gone. He gave his head a shake. *Must have been a mirage—a trick of the mind. A trick of the light. There's no light left in the universe. None—except Billie's glow stick.*

There was another flash, so quick he almost missed it.

That's it! It's got to be!

Sherman sprang to his feet. He grabbed Billie by the shoulders and spun her around. He pointed into the darkness toward the speck of light. When her head swung round to face him, he knew by the look in her eye, she was thinking the same thing he was: *Go!*

Sherman snatched his violin case and raced in the direction of the sparkle of light. Every second or two he saw it again, leading him toward it like a signal. He trod gingerly over the precious Spirit Stones, having the distinct feeling he was walking over something that was somehow alive. He stumbled several times, falling flat into a heap almost feeling like tiny hands of pure energy were helping him to his feet.

It was slow going, like crossing an ocean of bowling balls and though his mind told him he needed to hurry, Sherman's body had trouble responding to the challenge. *Can you run out of time, if you're in a place without time? Will there be some kind of warning, or will the wormhole just snap shut? Am I already too late to save Drake and Stella? If they are in the past and the Earth is in the future, then where am I? What time am I in? Am I in time or out of it...or somewhere in between?* Sherman's mind was a ball of confusion, but he used the adrenaline to press himself onward.

With each step closer, the tiny flicker of light began to grow in intensity, until finally he had to shield his eyes. With his head bent he scaled a mountain of Spirit Stones with Billie right by his side. He was almost at the top and risked a glance upward, but the light was so bright, he had to shield his eyes with both hands. He dropped his violin case and lost his balance. The mountain rumbled and like a stack of gumballs came crashing down scattering in all directions. Sherman rolled in one direction and Billie in the other, but luckily the Spirit Stone they had been searching for remained on top of the heap.

Sherman lunged for the stone. He grasped it, turned it over in his hands. He could barely look at it as the particle of light filling the small hole was so bright, but he did catch a glimpse of the inscription. This one was in a language he clearly understood and the letters read simply: Stella Livingstone. He closed his eyes and ran his hands over the stone, feeling for the spot where the missing piece belonged.

Suddenly, he could see Stella's face before him. Her friendly smile. Her crystal blue eyes. He could even smell her fruity shampoo. Drake hated that smell. He'd go on and on about how his sister smelled like a giant kiwi. It was as though Sherman could feel Stella's very essence, as though he was holding her soul in the palm of his hand.

Sherman motioned for Billie to toss him the pendant. As she let it fly, she lost her balance and tumbled down an embankment of Spirit Stones. Sherman managed to snatch the pendant out of the air. He couldn't worry about Billie. Not now. There was no time. He had to finish the task before it was too late. With trembling hands he pressed as hard as he could but there was something stuck inside the hole in the Spirit Stone preventing Stella's pendant from snapping into the gap.

Sherman pushed with all his might and suddenly, a glimmer of light squeezed out. It reocketed upward like a drop of crystal set on fire. Sherman watched as the light soared high into the air and then plummeted downward into the center of the lake. The lake lit up for one brief moment and then the light disappeared into the depths of the still water.

In that same instant, the missing piece clicked in place like the last piece of an intricate puzzle. The Spirit Stone was whole again.

chapter twenty-six

"You have done well, Drake," said Umbra coldly. "Now take your place beside me for all eternity."

Drake's face was twisted with hate as the barrier he'd created to block his thoughts and emotions exploded. His plan to save Stella had failed. He had thought if he could release her from the capsule, her light would destroy Umbra and they could find a way home. Now it was by his own hand that his sister was gone. His hand— spurred on by the evil will of Umbra.

"It's all your fault!" he screamed, lunging for the monstrous figure. "You made me do it!"

"No Drake, I am afraid you are wrong," said Umbra side-stepping the wild attempt to tackle him. Drake hit the wall of the Obelisk and fell flat on his back.

"Everything you have done, you have done of your own free will," said Umbra. "It was your hand and your heart that completed the task. But come, come. Do not grieve her loss. In time you will come to accept your fate—perhaps even enjoy it. Now once and for all, darkness—not light—rules the universe."

Drake was about to scramble to his feet to attack Umbra again, when a blistering pain seared his eyes shut and forced him back to the ground. He managed to open his eyes a sliver. Everything was happening all at once, so quickly, and yet his brain was registering everything in slow motion.

Up through the hole in Stella's heart rose a speck of light, so tiny, yet so powerful he had to shield his eyes. As the granule of light rose higher and higher the walls of the Obelisk were set on fire. Soon light with the strength of a million suns emanated from all around. Shadowbands shrieked and squealed as they exploded one by one into nothingness.

The light pierced though Umbra, illuminating his black figure. Drake saw a burning skeleton shining right through the black garb. Umbra screeched as though the light were cutting him.

"We are separated," said a wispy voice Drake had never heard before. It was soft and airy like the wind. More like a whispering inside his head. Though it was horribly painful, he risked a glance upward and saw that the speck of light had grown into the delicate silhouette of a woman swathed and shimmering in pure white light.

"Aura," he whispered.

"Yes," she responded. Then she held her palm down toward the body of Stella. "Behold your sister, Drake. She has served me well. She has fulfilled her destiny as you have yours."

Drake watched as the hole in Stella sealed itself as though someone were replacing the missing piece. The only evidence left behind was a rip in her ski jacket from the sword.

"No!" shrieked Umbra, his voice strained with panic and rage. "Not again! You will not steal my triumph out from under me! It is you that should die! You! Not I!"

"No, brother," said the lady of light. "I knew your plan before you knew it yourself. I hid a piece of myself inside this poor creature's Spirit Stone. She was part of me and I part of her. I knew you would come to destroy me one day but I was prepared."

"I was prepared too!" he shrieked. "I knew what you had done! The shell you housed yourself in was weak. I had only to destroy *her* and you would die along with her."

"It was a good plan, dear brother. But what

you did not know was that your young learner," she pointed to Drake, "would send out another and that one would undo the connection in time. Stella and I were separated before the blade came down, and I used your sword to cut the silk tomb you had spun for me and open the tunnel to let out my light. Ultimately it was *you*, your jealousy and your hatred that has caused your demise."

Umbra, now shriveling and writhing in pain, his very being smoldering to nothing, let out a cry that forced Drake's hands to his ears. Drake shut his eyes from the light and stood deaf and blind to the commotion around him. Umbra mumbled one last thing that sounded like, "So, you had it all planned? But I'll wager you did not plan on this!"

Drake felt a hard jerk on his leg and as Umbra began to shrivel into nothingness, he felt the grip tighten and he felt himself being dragged downward. Shriveling. Shrinking. Disappearing along with Umbra...

Stella opened her eyes just in time to see her brother fading along with Umbra. She screamed, and grabbed hold of Drake's arm yanking with all her might. But he was somehow attached to Umbra and Umbra was vanishing.

chapter twenty-seven

Billie rolled out of control, bumping and bouncing to the bottom of the Gorge. She dropped the glow stick, but it didn't matter because in that instant there was suddenly light—bright beaming light emanating from the pool in the center of the Gorge.

When she hit the stones, Drake's clock jarred itself loose from her pocket. It flew through the air, struck a cluster of Spirit Stones and shattered like glass. The rattling she had heard inside it all along was suddenly revealed. Inside the clock there was another piece of a Spirit Stone—the same size as the one that had been Stella's.

Billie scooped up the fragment and scrambled toward Sherman. He was still holding Stella's completed Spirit Stone.

Billie handed Sherman the stone that had been stuck inside Drake's clock. Sherman understood instantly. *That's why we had to bring Drake's clock along!*

They both began digging frantically through the pile of stones looking for the one that housed Drake's spirit.

It can't be far from his twin sister's, Sherman reasoned. *It's got to be here somewhere.*

Tossing stones aside left, right and center, Sherman felt a sudden tremble in the Gorge.

Oh no! It's the doorway! It's snapping shut!

"Get *et et* out *out out!*" Sherman yelled to Billie, but she shook her head and kept on digging.

A second rumble shook the canyon like an earthquake. The last of the white dwarves had to be leaving. The machine would be grinding to a halt and the doorway would be closing forever.

Just as Sherman had abandoned all hope, he reached down and pulled up a Spirit Stone. On it was the inscription: Drake Hamilton Livingstone. Sherman quickly snapped in the piece and felt icy darkness ooze out of it. Something had been stuck inside Drake and whatever it was, it hadn't been good. Without a second to spare, Sherman dropped the stone and raced for Billie, scooping up his violin case as he ran.

He grabbed Billie and hauled her toward the pool at the center of the Gorge. They had to follow the light. Sherman knew it was the only way out of the black hole.

He pushed Billie into the water, shouting, "Swim *im im!*"

Sherman, still clutching his violin case, dove in after Billie. Pumping as hard as he could, he kicked and splashed toward her, grabbing her and pulling her down under the water. At first she wrestled him frantically and he realized she didn't understand—they had to get to the bottom before there was no more bottom. He couldn't hold her with one arm. He had to make a choice. It was his violin or Billie.

He let the instrument drift away as he yanked her beneath the surface.

chapter twenty-eight

Drake tumbled back into his sister's arms. He felt as though a slimy darkness was oozing out of his body and mind and, for the first time, he felt free of Umbra.

"No!" cried the monster as he began to fade. "You are mine! You are my *Evil Darking Stone...*" Drake watched Umbra evaporate in a puff of black smoke. He turned to face the sister he thought he'd lost a second time.

"Stella!" Drake choked back a wave of emotion. He flung himself upon her and hugged her so tight she began to cough. "You're alive!"

Stella grinned wildly. "I knew you wouldn't give up on me, Drake. I knew you'd come back for me."

He hugged her again.

"I was counting on it too," said the voice of Aura. Drake looked up at a specter of light glowing above them. Then he heard another voice. He froze. *Impossible...Could it be?*

Out of the hole in the floor where the sword had crashed through, crawled Sherman Glutz, followed by someone else Drake didn't recognize.

"Come on Billie, you can do it. Breathe. Just breathe. We made it. We're through."

"Sherman!" Drake yelled as he raced toward his friend. He hurled himself on top of Sherman, knocking the two of them onto the floor. Stella followed, jumping onto the pile.

"You did it! You figured things out! You *are* a genius! A real genius! But...how did you get *here*? And who is *that*?" Drake pointed to Billie who was still catching her breath.

"Drake! Stella!" Sherman's enthusiasm swelled and then dwindled as he searched his surroundings. "Where are we? Are we home?"

"We're not home, Sherman," said Stella. "We're inside the Crystal Obelisk on the Bright Side of the Halfstone. How did you get here?"

Sherman looked at the girl, who he'd once thought to be nothing more than a figment of his friend's imagination. Not only was her body real, but he'd held her Spirit Stone in the palm of his hands.

"I went through a Wormhole—a tunnel in time and space. One end was in the clock in my bedroom, and the other end came out here."

"You completed your task, Sherman," said Aura, her voice raining sparks upon his head. "Because of you, your friends are safe and my light has returned."

Sherman shielded his eyes stealing a glance at the slight figure of a woman enveloped in swirls of pure white light. She was the most magnificent thing he'd ever seen. He blushed in her radiance. He grabbed hold of Billie's shoulders and swung her around. "We did it, Billie! We saved them!"

"Save your celebratin', Worm," grinned Billie. "It doesn't look like this is over yet."

"She is right," said Aura. "You must all return now. The shadow is passing. Once it is completely gone, it will be too late."

"But how?" asked Stella.

"You came through a tunnel of light. Now you will exit through one."

It happened suddenly as though the Obelisk was inverted. Drake felt himself falling upward, sliding through the tunnel of light faster and faster.

chapter twenty-nine

Drake lay on his back in the snow, looking up at the sky through his Sherman Shields. *What happened? Where am I?*

The last piece of moon slipped past the surface of the sun, letting the light shine fully once again.

Drake sat bolt upright—an action that set his head spinning. He steadied it with both hands. His gloves were missing and his fingers were cold. Stella lay on her back beside him. There was a large rip in her jacket over her heart.

"I just had one crazy dream," said Sherman, pulling off his hunter's hat and rubbing his head. He looked down at his feet. "Hey! Where are my boots? And why is my left foot *red*?"

"It wasn't a dream," whispered Stella. "It's just starting to fade like one."

Drake looked around at the tight circle of cedars that surrounded him. Light reflected off the crisp snow making him feel as though he were swimming in a sea of silver. He removed his Sherman Shields.

"It really happened...didn't it?" he asked.

But even as he spoke, he could feel everything slipping behind a curtain of haze in his mind. It was all bleeding together like a giant wet watercolor. Smearing. Smudging. Fading. He closed his eyes and took a deep breath. "Umbra is finally gone."

"No," said Stella. "Not gone. He can never be gone. Not completely. You can't kill the darkness any more than you can kill light. And besides, would you really want to?"

Stella had a point. And yet, it was no comfort to Drake. "Then, he's still part of me," he sighed.

"No," whispered Stella. "Sherman broke the connection. We're free."

Drake shook his head. He fixed his sister with a helpless stare. "You may be free, but no matter what, I'll always be the *Evil Darking Stone*."

Stella's voice seemed to fill the entire clearing. "No, Drake. You never were."

Tears spilled down Drake's cheeks. "I am," he insisted. "Even my name spells it out."

Stella looked at her brother and smiled. "Not exactly."

She stood up and moved to a clear patch of snow. There, she traced Drake's name with her hand. She looked at her brother as if to say, *watch this*. Then she turned back and inserted his middle name so that the inscription read:

Drake Hamilton Livingstone

Drake shrugged. "So? What does that prove?"

"Just wait."

One by one Stella cancelled out the letters of Drake's name and rearranged them on a fresh patch of snow. He watched in amazement, as the words took shape. Instead of *Evil Darking Stone*, the letters now spelled:

One Light Into Man's Vile Dark

Drake read it aloud. He paused, and then read it again. He frowned.

"You see, Drake," said Stella, "you never were the *Evil Darking Stone*. Umbra was wrong. That's why his plan failed. You were not the *darkness*. You were the *light*. I wasn't the *chosen one* after all. It was you. It was always you—the *One Light*."

She extended her hand toward her brother and waited.

Drake sat for a moment letting it all sink in. So much had happened. He'd lived a lifetime in the one minute of the eclipse's totality. Time and Space now had new meaning for him. They weren't separate. And they weren't one. They spiraled around and around each other.

He looked at Stella; she was smiling.

He had always been so jealous of her. He'd spent his whole life resenting her and now suddenly those feelings were gone. He reached out, grasped her hand and squeezed hard as she pulled him to his feet.

Sherman looked around as though he were searching for something. "Someone's missing."

Drake looked puzzled. "Who?"

"I'm not sure. Wasn't there someone else with us?"

Drake looked at Stella. Stella shrugged her shoulders.

Everything was fading quickly now. It was leaving their memories like the shadow of the moon had left the earth.

"Come on," said Stella. "Let's get back to school."

"Right," said Drake, pulling Sherman to his

feet and grabbing his backpack. "Mrs Oxman is probably going nuts looking for us."

"We'll have to explain everything," said Stella.

"Explain what?" asked Sherman.

"Beats me," shrugged Drake.

They left the circle of cedar trees and walked back to the school side by side.

MARINA COHEN is an elementary school teacher with the York Region District School Board. She has a Master's Degree in French Literature from the University of Toronto. Marina has always been fascinated by notions of time and space. Her treasured Moon Phases clock, which features prominently in this novel, hangs proudly on the wall in her home in Markham, Ontario, where she lives with her husband and three children.

Trick of the Light is the sequel to Marina's first book, *Shadow of the Moon*.

For comprehensive teachers' guides visit

www.marinacohen.com